"Della!"

Erin's gaze swung to the woman who had shouted. She was decked out in a sleeveless satin gown and long pearls similar to the ones Della had been wearing. The woman handed her cocktail to the waiter and rushed forward, the long feather in her glittery headband bobbing.

"It *is* you! Wherever have you been? Oh, good Lord, you're bleeding!" The woman grasped Erin's arm, giving Erin's denim shirt and jeans a puzzled look. "What in heaven's name have you done to yourself?"

"You," she instructed the waiter, who was gaping at Erin, "close your mouth and get J.B. over here!"

Erin shook her head and ran a shaky hand through her hair. "I'm...uh—I'm not who you think—"

The woman disregarded her. "J.B., there you are! Just look at Della! And look at the blood on..."

Erin looked up. My God, it was *him!*

Dear Readers,

I'm often asked where I get my ideas. That question has many answers, depending on which book one might wonder about. *The Locket* was inspired by a trip to the Marland Mansion in Ponca City, Oklahoma. It is a magnificent home, open for tours, and was built by the tenth governor of Oklahoma, oil baron E. W. Marland. The history behind the mansion is fascinating, and my imagination went wild as I toured Mr. Marland's grand home. Though my characters inhabit a similar mansion, in a small town much like Ponca City, Oklahoma, the tale I've told is fictional, of course. The real-life folks were quite interesting, don't get me wrong, but I'm rather fond of creating my own. I hope you'll enjoy *The Locket* and find the era as romantic and wondrous as I did.

Sincerely,

Brenna Todd

Brenna Todd
The Locket

Harlequin Books

TORONTO • NEW YORK • LONDON
AMSTERDAM • PARIS • SYDNEY • HAMBURG
STOCKHOLM • ATHENS • TOKYO • MILAN
MADRID • WARSAW • BUDAPEST • AUCKLAND

This one's for you, Mom. Because you love time travels, and you didn't take me to a psychiatrist because of the imaginary dogs.

ISBN 0-373-70621-9

THE LOCKET

ABOUT THE AUTHOR

Golden Heart winner Brenna Todd likes a challenge. Each book she writes has a new yet distinctive flavor. Her heroes and heroines are men and women you could meet on the street—or on an adventure that takes you back in time. *The Locket* is just such a story, based on her winning approach—adding a magic "what if" to a real-life event, and then, of course, including a healthy dose of romance to keep readers hungry for more.

Brenna lives in Oklahoma with her husband and two children.

Books by Brenna Todd

HARLEQUIN SUPERROMANCE

Don't miss any of our special offers. Write to us at the following address for information on our newest releases.

Harlequin Reader Service
U.S.: 3010 Walden Ave., P.O. Box 1325, Buffalo, NY 14269
Canadian: P.O. Box 609, Fort Erie, Ont. L2A 5X3

ACKNOWLEDGMENTS

Without help from the following people, this book would not have been possible. I am deeply grateful, and will apologize now for taking "artistic license" with the facts you gave me.

Cliff Vermillion, of the Marland Mansion in Ponca City, Oklahoma, who took me and my video camera through the tunnels.

Judy Johnson, librarian at the Ponca City Library, who helped with the history of her region of the state.

Genevieve and Roy Higgins, my own dear grandparents, who "remembered the days" with me.

Joyce Anglin and Kathie Compton. Thank you, Joyce, for "the shadow." Thank you, Kathie, for the handy-dandy reference manual.

My virtual critique group and on-line buddies. You are all wonders! Special thanks go to Monica Catalbano for resurrecting Erin's father, and Judith Tarr, Callie Goble and all other horse experts.

James Davis of EMSA of Tulsa, for his knowledge of all things paramedic, and David "Doc Danger" Brockway for the information on heart attacks.

CHAPTER ONE

"UNIT TWO, PRIORITY-ONE chest pains. Your patient is an elderly male reported to be pale and diaphoretic. He is conscious and breathing with some respiratory difficulty. Patient has a cardiac history. See the caretaker of Munro estate, 300 West Munro Boulevard."

Erin Sawyer watched Chuck, her partner of two weeks, flip on the lights and throw the unit into Drive. As they shot into traffic, siren wailing, he whistled long and low. "That's old J. B. Munro."

Erin didn't question the fact that her partner knew who their patient was. He knew everyone in this town of twelve thousand. But then, so did everyone else in Munro, Oklahoma. Most were even related.

"City founder," Chuck commented over the blare of the siren as they wove through the sparse morning traffic. "He's Oklahoma's own version of a Rockefeller. He was a railroad magnate who planned and built Munro. Gotta be a hundred years old if he's a day."

"Subaru at two o'clock," Erin warned, and Chuck swerved deftly to avoid the small car. Then he punched the accelerator and whizzed through an intersection.

Chuck glanced sideways at her. "Guess this is more like what you're used to."

"What?"

"Well, you've been on the job here two weeks now and the most thrilling thing we've done is rescue Old Man Hixon's fat basset hound from that killer log he got stuck in," Chuck said with a grin.

Erin laughed. "You call that exciting?"

"Was for Hixon's dog." Chuck slowed for a corner. "Lots of exciting stuff in Detroit, huh?"

Erin nodded and watched as they whizzed by small, quiet homes. She missed the adrenaline rush, the excitement of being a paramedic in Detroit, where nearly every call had been a life-and-death situation. But it was difficult explaining that to the other paramedics in Munro. They just smiled and shook their heads whenever she discussed big-city emergency calls, then proudly quoted their nearly nonexistent crime stats. There hadn't been a murder in Munro in ten years. Three had been committed in the preceding fifty. Liquor stores weren't robbed. Car-jacking and street corner drug deals were unheard of. The only rival gangs in Munro were the two quilting circles—one at the First

Methodist Church and one at the Free Will Baptist.

"The slower pace here will be good for Mom and Pop," she told Chuck. For her, too. She'd just keep telling herself that until she believed it. "They grew up here."

"Did your daddy ever tell you about J.B.? The scandal?"

"No. I think it was always painful for him to talk about Oklahoma. He missed it so much." But he was home now, and on the mend, recovering from a near-fatal heart attack.

"What was the scandal about?" she asked.

"Well—this was years and years ago, mind you, back in the twenties—J.B. and his first wife, Virginia, took in her poor relatives' daughter to raise. Made her their ward.

"Virginia died eight or nine years later, and old J.B. waited about a year, then took the ward as his second wife. She was only eighteen or so at the time. Name was Della."

Erin raised a brow. "Married the girl he was raising? I'm surprised the good citizens of Munro didn't change the name of their town."

Chuck grinned. "But that was only the half of it. Della was murdered some years later and they never found out who killed her. Rumor had it she was fooling around with J.B.'s business partner and the partner did her in. But some suspect it was J.B. himself, since he didn't take kindly to their little affair."

Within minutes they arrived at the huge estate Erin had seen from the road several times since moving to Munro, and Chuck turned down the tree-lined drive. Though it was now a small farming community, Munro had once boasted an impressive number of millionaires who'd struck it rich in oil. Some of them had built homes on the land surrounding J.B.'s, but his residence greatly overshadowed theirs in size and magnificence.

It stood proudly amid tangled vines and unclipped shrubbery, looking more like King Arthur's castle than a railroad entrepreneur's mansion. Turrets were positioned at all four corners of the stone facade, and stone-carved griffins snarled from each of its four stories. A huge coat of arms emblazoned with the name Munro hung next to a set of heavy wooden doors. But for the lack of a drawbridge and moat, the place made Erin feel as though she'd stepped onto British soil.

"It's something else, isn't it?" Chuck observed, his awe and pride unabashed.

"Yes. Looks like it could use a regular gardener, though."

"Oh, sure, it could stand a little sprucing up, but in its day this place was a showcase. The townsfolk called it the Palace on the Prairie. They'd never seen anything like it out here.''

Chuck pulled the unit to a stop under the portico that shaded the front steps, and Erin grabbed her kit, then swung out of the van. He passed her as she vaulted up the stairs. "Looks deserted, doesn't it?" he said, as he reached the door and pounded the heavy wrought-iron knocker. Stopping next to Chuck, Erin waited in silence while he tried to open the door. Finding it locked, he banged the knocker harder, then harder still. With a frown, Chuck leaned over and pounded on a window beside the door. "EMS!" he shouted. "Can someone let us in?"

Bracketing her eyes with her palms, Erin peered through the window on her side of the door. All the furniture was covered with sheets. No lights shone in any of the rooms. "There's no one in there." She stepped back. "It looks all closed up. Think he could be upstairs?"

"Could be. But you'd think the caretaker would be on the lookout for us." Chuck turned and started down the steps. "I'm going to call Dispatch to reconfirm," he said over his shoulder.

Erin made for the doors again, banging the knocker and still getting no response. She darted down the steps and circled the house, trying each ground-level window, shouting Mr. Munro's name every few seconds. When she returned to the front steps, she noticed Chuck was still in the van, waiting for the reconfirm. Frustrated, she headed for the doors one last time.

But at the top step she froze, overcome by a sense of foreboding. She shivered as she heard an eerie humming sound. Staring at the double doors, she focused her gaze on the faint carvings just below the iron knocker. A Celtic design surrounded an ornate set of initials: J.B.M. Despite her inexplicable uneasiness, she stepped forward, unaccountably compelled to touch the carvings.

When the pads of her fingers made contact with the wood, she experienced a strange sense of déjà vu. How bizarre. She'd seen this house from the road, but had never set foot on the property. So why did she feel as if she'd touched these doors before?

Could she have seen the house closer up as a child? She and her family had made plenty of summer trips to Munro to visit relatives. Maybe she'd seen them then—

"He's in the guesthouse!"

Erin swiveled to stare in Chuck's direction. Guesthouse—? Instantly her presence of mind returned, and Erin raced down the steps. Hopping into the passenger seat, she buckled herself in.

Chuck didn't even glance her way as he threw the van into Drive and sped off to the back corner of the estate.

"HURRY! HE'S RIGHT in there, sittin' on the couch."

Erin and Chuck rushed past the elderly gentleman standing in the doorway of the guesthouse. He followed them inside. "I check on him every day. Every day without fail he's up and around, just a-blowin' and a-goin'. But not today. He . . . he's in a bad way."

And he was. J.B. Munro's skin had the sickly gray pallor of someone who had suffered a heart attack, and his lined face was contorted with a pain-induced grimace. His thin white hair was slicked down with perspiration, and his clothes were soaked with it. He clutched his chest with an age-withered hand.

Chuck hurriedly set up an oxygen unit and hooked Munro to the heart monitor. Erin fastened a blood-pressure cuff around his arm.

"Mr. Munro, we're with EMS," she said as she checked his pressure and pulse. She shot Chuck a look indicating her findings were not good. "We're here to help you, sir. Can you talk to me at all?"

A tortured moan was her only answer.

Chuck flipped on the monitor and Erin winced inwardly when she heard the weak rhythm of Munro's heart. It matched the pressure and pulse reading she'd just taken.

Grabbing a sterile package from her kit, Erin glanced up at Chuck again. "Need to start a line with D5W." She ripped open the package and extracted a catheter. Tying a tourniquet around Munro's thin arm, she searched for a vein. Chuck squatted down next to her as she hooked the IV tubing to the catheter. When she'd taped down the tubing, Chuck found the site with a hypodermic, then pushed the plunger.

"Stretcher," Chuck said, then sprinted away to get it.

Erin reached into her kit for a small towel, then dabbed at the perspiration on Mr. Munro's forehead. He groaned again, and Erin's heart went out to him. Poor thing, he was so old. Chuck's estimate was probably right; the man had to be at least a hundred. He looked so frail, and as vulnerable as a child. A peculiar C-shaped scar near his left eye gleamed silver, and his eyes mirrored the shock and fear that had been in her father's the night he'd nearly died. She felt shaky at the thought and began talking to J.B. again to erase the memory.

"I'm with EMS, Mr. Munro," she repeated. "My partner and I are going to take you to the hospital."

He looked at her then, his pained expression giving way to one of confusion. A slight frown creased his brow and he mouthed a word over and over again—one that Erin couldn't make out.

She gave him a reassuring smile. "Don't be afraid, sir. You're going to be all right," she said, wiping his brow again. "Just lie as still as possible and—"

"Della?" he muttered, lifting a trembling hand to her cheek. "My God . . . it's you, Della."

"No, Mr. Munro," she said gently, lowering his hand to his side. Disorientation was another symptom of a heart attack. Her father had done the same kind of thing—looked straight into Erin's eyes and called her by her mother's name.

"I'm with EMS and—"

"Still so beautiful," he said, his voice rusty as a solitary tear wet the C-shaped scar, then rolled down his ashen cheek. "My beautiful Della."

She didn't know why, but Erin suddenly felt uneasy. The look of recognition in Munro's eyes seemed so lucid. "No, Mr. Munro, I'm—"

"Can you forgive me, Della? You know I never meant to hurt—" His voice cracked and more tears came. He found her hand with his and squeezed it, surprising Erin with the strength of his grip.

"What I did to you—" His agitation made his already difficult breathing worsen. "Dear God, what I did—"

Erin wiped the tears away with the towel. "It's okay, Mr. Munro. Everything's going to be fine." She slipped her hand out of his. "Just lie still, please. Calm down and lie still."

He did as he was told, but the tears didn't stop. And through his tears, his gaze was trained on Erin with such intensity that a shiver darted up her spine. She jumped when he grasped her hand again and tried to sit up.

"No. No, I was wrong!" he exclaimed. "You're not Della."

"Calm down, Mr. Munro, please. You're going to tear out this IV."

"You're not Della."

"That's right," she replied in a placating tone. "I'm—"

"You don't have to tell me. I know who you are," he whispered. "You're the other one. You're Erin."

THE DOORS OF THE emergency room whooshed open and Erin walked through, leaving the placid, star-sprinkled Munro night to enter the deserted hospital wing.

What a difference several hours made. No swarm of doctors and nurses hovering at the entrance. No tension, no anxiety hanging in the air. Now the only sound was the faint hum of overhead lights and air-conditioning.

As always, Erin and her partner had immediately relinquished their patient to the hospital staff. The only difference was that the man they'd left this morning had paid for the building of this hospital. And he had known her name.

Coincidence, Chuck had said. Erin was new to Munro. She hadn't even heard of J. B. Munro before today. The poor old guy had been out of his head, mumbling names from his past. He'd called out to his dead wife, hadn't he? He had probably known an Erin, too. The name was not uncommon.

Erin paced in front of the desk, her crepe-soled shoes squeaking on the waxed floor. Though the thermostat was kept in the low seventies, she felt chilled.

She shoved her hands into the pockets of her uniform slacks, then jerked them out again to rub her upper arms briskly. Taking a seat in the waiting area, she checked her watch, hoping that Janeen, the night nurse, wouldn't take a longer-than-usual coffee break.

Leaning her head back and closing her eyes, Erin thought of another night, another hospital. Only then, she'd been waiting for news of her father.

Sometimes it seemed as if a million years had passed since Pop's attack. Other times, it seemed as if it had happened only yesterday. She could still hear his pleading. "Take me home, Erin," he'd said in a broken voice. "I can't rest in this place if I die. I need to go home." And Erin had vowed to herself she would take him home, all right, but not to bury him; she'd promised herself that she would see him completely recuperated in the tiny Oklahoma town where he and his wife had grown up.

It was the least Erin could do. She was an only child, born late in her parents' lives after countless years of attempting to conceive. She'd been the center of their existence, showered with love and blessed with a sense of security that few of her friends had ever known. And she'd be damned if she would see those two beloved people spend their golden years in a city where they'd become afraid to walk the streets. Every time she recalled the image of her father lying in that hospital bed, and her mother wringing her hands as she stood by, Erin knew that she would give up anything and everything to see to their happiness.

So she had made some sacrifices. She'd left behind good friends, an exciting job and an active social life in Detroit, not to mention a man whom she'd almost been convinced was "the one." But if Brian had been, he would have understood, and would have waited for her instead of becoming engaged to someone else. She'd quickly realized she was better off without him.

"Erin . . . ? Why, it *is* you."

Erin sat up, shoving thoughts of Brian away to smile at the short, matronly nurse. Her tightly permed hair was pulled back in a banana clip behind a cluster of curls at her forehead that bounced with every step she took. "Hi, Janeen."

"You can't be pulling a double shift," she said, grinning at Erin as she walked behind the desk. "No such thing as doubles in little old Munro."

"You're right," Erin replied with a chuckle as she walked toward her. "I'm just here to check on J.B."

Janeen's grin faded, and she shook her head slowly. "We did everything we could, but the poor old guy didn't make it."

Erin couldn't find her voice for a moment. She felt cold inside—a deep, hollow sense of loss she couldn't explain. "He . . . died?"

Janeen nodded. "Had another attack, hon. Massive, this time."

The chill deepened, and Erin frowned, not understanding why she felt such intense sadness. She had spent less than an hour of her life with J. B. Munro. There was no logical reason for Erin to feel anything but simple regret. Still, tears pooled in her eyes, then streaked down her face.

"Oh, hon..." Janeen said, blinking with surprise. She circled the desk and placed a comforting arm around Erin's shoulder, her curly bangs tickling Erin's chin. "You're taking this awfully hard, aren't you?"

How could she explain to Janeen what she couldn't explain to herself? "I think it's— Well, I think it must be because he reminded me of my father. I don't know if you'd heard about my pop's heart attack in Detroit—"

"Munro's a small town. We all knew his complete medical history about five minutes after you hit town." Janeen smiled kindly and gave Erin's shoulders another squeeze. "But old J.B. lived a long, full life. Goodness, he was a hundred and seven, did you know that? Much older than your daddy."

Erin dashed the backs of her hands across her cheeks. "I know, and I feel so... silly, crying for someone I don't even know."

"You shouldn't." Janeen blinked back a few tears herself. "I think it's touching, in fact. And I'll tell you what else I think. It's a bunch of baloney, all that 'maintain a professional distance' stuff. If we didn't care, we would have chosen another sort of career. Besides, even though the whole town will make a big to-do about J.B.'s passing, there's no one left who'll shed real tears, is there, now?"

Erin sniffed. Her throat felt raw and her eyes swollen and hot, as though she'd been crying for hours. "No family, you mean?"

"No family. No friends. Unless you count the man who let you and Chuck in this morning. And he's just a paid employee, from what I understand." Janeen patted her arm, then walked back behind the desk, still eyeing Erin with concern. "And don't you think J.B. wasn't grateful for the compassion you showed him on his last day, Erin. He must have sensed how much you cared, hon."

"What do you mean?"

"Well, he mentioned your name to me. They moved him to the cardiac-care unit, of course, but it was slow down here so I checked on him a few times. He was conscious on one of my visits." A melancholy smile pulled at the corners of her mouth, and she reached for the phone that had begun to ring. Picking up the receiver, her index finger hovered over the lighted-up button for a moment. "I think he plans to thank you again...if you wind up in the same place," she said with a wink. "He told me to tell you someday you'd know why he was so grateful."

CHAPTER TWO

SHE HEARD HER MOTHER'S Buick pull into the drive. Two car doors opened, then closed. The muffled sounds of her mother's and Aunt Shirley's voices drifted through the screen door. Erin looked up from her magazine, smiling at the women's chatter. Her father shifted in the rented hospital bed.

"Wonder how many antique shops they wiped out this time," he grumbled good-naturedly.

"Well, good morning," Erin said with a chuckle, since it was actually late afternoon. She set down her magazine and crossed the room. It had been two months since his second heart attack, the one he'd suffered shortly after Mr. Munro's death, and Hank Sawyer was still recuperating. His sleep cycle was still irregular. He tossed and turned at night, then slept during the day. Nor had he regained enough strength, in Erin's opinion.

"Don't know why you aren't out there helping bolster the economy with them."

Erin laughed, lifting her father's arm to take his pulse. "Can't keep up with them. Those two take their shopping seriously."

He grinned again. "You ought to be out doing something, though. Young woman like you shouldn't have to waste your time sitting in a sickroom all day."

"Stop that," she said gently. "If I wanted to be anywhere else, do anything else, I'd be out doing it, wouldn't I?"

"Don't know about that."

Erin ignored his comment like she always did. Lately he'd been complaining a lot about her spending so much time with him.

The screen door opened. Her mother and Aunt Shirley bustled in, loaded down with sacks and packages. At her father's groan, Erin smiled.

"Do the words *fixed income* mean nothing to you, woman?" Hank said to his wife.

Shirley laughed and Dorothea Sawyer gave her husband a look of mock annoyance. "You always were tighter than the bark on a tree," she chided, setting down her haul on the living room sofa and making her way over to the bed. She dropped a kiss on his cheek. "Your color's better than usual," she stated, then looked up at Erin. "You going to let him up and around soon?"

"I think so." Although his restlessness at night still bothered Erin, her mother needed reassurance. The stress would begin to affect her health soon, and Erin didn't want both her parents in a fragile state. "But no power shopping with *you*," she added. "Not for another year, at least."

Her mother grinned and reached for her husband's hand, lacing her fingers through his. "I'll give up the binges the minute he's out of this bed."

Hank's laugh was spirited. "There's incentive!"

Dorothea patted his arm. "He's getting better, all right." She turned to Erin. "Are you gonna love what I bought you! I found the most beautiful locket for you in an antique shop. Come over here and see—"

"Can't that wait, Dorothea?" Aunt Shirley interrupted. "I was hoping Erin would take a break. Maybe go with me to Braum's for a cup of coffee or something."

"Oh, yes, that's a good idea. Shirley, make sure you talk to her about getting back to Detroit soon. You weren't supposed to have been here this long in the first place, child. We're taking advantage, I think—"

"Mom, you're not," Erin argued, struggling not to show her impatience. Her parents had broached this particular subject too many times already. Now her mother had brought Aunt Shirley into it.

"Have you ever known me to do something I didn't want to do? If Pop hadn't had the second attack, I would have left sooner. You know that."

"Oh, we know it, all right. You've been an independent little cuss since the day you were born," Hank said, a thread of pride in his voice. "But you were also born to take care of people. You've always jumped at the chance to nurse every stray animal in the vicinity, every sick friend. It's no wonder you chose to go into medicine."

"Pop," she protested, shaking her head, "you're hardly a stray, and I think you can see it's my place to—"

"Well, that's just it, honey." Hank took her hand in his. "We think you're taking your responsibility to us too far. It's not that we don't appreciate it, but it's time you got on with your own life."

Her mom spoke up. "Your father's right. You've always been a caregiver, but maybe we've depended on you more than we should. And this past year, well, you've given up far too much to care for us. We know you did it out of love, but we want you to be happy, too."

Erin looked from parent to parent, her frown marring her smooth brow. "I haven't given up all that much. I'm still a paramedic, and I plan to return to Detroit once Pop's health improves."

"It's not the same, Erin," her mother said, "being a paramedic here rather than in Detroit. We know that. Much as we didn't like you being in dangerous situations from time to time, we knew you thrived on the excitement. And we accepted it."

"Okay, granted…it's not the same." Erin moved away from her father's bed, dragging a hand through her hair in frustration. "But you've given me so much over the years. Why won't you let *me* help *you* now? It'll be easy enough to pick up my life in Detroit again, once you're better," she assured them.

"We think you should do it now, Erin."

Erin shook her head. "No, Pop. I'll know when the time is right for me to leave. If you hadn't had the second attack—"

"But I did," he said. "And I could have another one, and one after that. But if I take care of myself and take it easy, I probably won't. Even if I do, I won't have you postponing your life indefinitely. It's just not right, girl!"

"Pop, calm down," she said, alarmed at the bright flush in his cheeks. She strode back to the bed, and reached for his wrist to check his pulse.

"Cut that out." He pulled his arm back. "I'm still your father, not just your patient. And you're going to listen to me."

Erin blinked. She couldn't remember the last time he'd spoken in such a forceful tone. She was glad to hear it in a way, glad he was showing strength. But it also disconcerted her. And hurt. She only had her parents' best interests at heart.

She was even more surprised by her father's next statement. "You're not going to get your way this time, honey. Your mother and I have discussed this and come to the decision that we're throwing you out... for your own good."

"Throwing me out!" Erin sputtered. "But I don't want— And you're not well enough to—"

"Oh, yes, I am. And Shirley and your mother," he went on, his tone unyielding, "will help you pack."

"Help me pack?"

"That's what I said."

Erin's mother touched her arm, her eyes sympathetic. "Honey, don't take this the wrong way. We love having you here, but this is no good for you. You're young and vital, and until your father's health problems, you had a life."

"Mom!" Erin gave an incredulous laugh. "I have a life now!" She glanced over at her aunt. "Aunt Shirley, he's your brother. Talk some sense into them. You know this is only temporary. Just because I've taken some time to help out doesn't mean I've become some... some old maid who's still living with her parents!''

Shirley cleared her throat, looking decidedly uncomfortable. "Actually, hon, I was the one who brought this to their attention in the first place.''

"What!''

"Well, sweetie, you've started to resemble your cousin, Beth Ann. Thirty-six and never lived a day away from Chester and Louise, and... Well, it worried me. So I spoke up.''

"Oh, for heaven's sake! I am nothing like Beth Ann." To Erin it was laughable. Her cousin was attached at the hip to her parents.

"But you have to admit, Erin, you rarely take a night out to spend time with friends or even go shopping with your mom and me,'' Shirley put in quietly.

Erin threw her hands in the air and groaned. "Okay, okay. I'll get out more," she declared. "In fact, I'll go today, all right? I'll take in a movie or something. Would that make you all happy?''

But it appeared that it wouldn't. Her father's features showed he wasn't about to bend.

"Good idea. You could use a breather. But your mother and Shirley will be packing your belongings while you're out, sweetheart.''

ERIN FUMED AS SHE DROVE up and down the tiny town's main drag a short time later. She cursed under her breath and smacked the steering wheel for good measure. They were all too stubborn for their own good.

She turned down Munro Boulevard, knowing she would need at least another thirty minutes of solitude in order to cool down enough to face them again.

Okay, she told herself, so they were only thinking of her own good. She realized that. They were unselfish, caring people, and Erin had always appreciated that fact, but she knew what was best for them. She was simply going to take a firmer stand.

Congratulations...very parental of you, a small voice in her brain piped in, irritating her further.

She wasn't playing the parent here! she argued. She only wanted what was best for them.

So true, the voice commiserated. *What in the world came over them? The nerve of them—looking out for your welfare over their own!*

She grimaced, not enjoying this debate with her conscience. She fingered the locket her mother had given her just before she'd stormed out, guilt washing in and dousing her ire. Stopping for a traffic light, she sighed. What a predicament. She loved her parents, and wanted them healthy and whole....

Exactly what they wanted for her.

A car horn behind her sounded lightly, and Erin moved through the intersection, hating the indecision that had crept in to shake her resolve. As she approached the Munro estate, which had been opened recently for tours, Erin found herself turning down its long, tree-lined drive. No use continuing aimlessly through town, stewing over the whole thing, she decided. Maybe if she just got her mind off the matter for an hour or so, she could think it through more clearly. Besides, she'd been curious about J. B. Munro and his mansion ever since she'd first come here.

THE FEROCIOUS-LOOKING stone griffins that stood watch at the two front corners of the house clasped a huge red vinyl banner in their claws that read: Munro Mansion Now Open to the Public.

Erin tucked her wallet into the pocket of her jeans and locked up her car. Approaching the mansion, she noted that landscapers were restoring the grounds.

Three 1920s-vintage cars that were parked beneath the portico caught Erin's attention. So did the teenage boy who hovered nearby, wearing his baseball cap backward on his head, and an earring in one ear. The teenager trailed his fingers reverently over the driver's side door of the mint-condition Packard, then popped his head inside the window. Erin glanced in the other side.

"These are cool old cars, aren't they?" he said.

"Yes." She found herself trying to picture J.B. as a young man, tooling along in this beauty. It wasn't easy. The image of J.B. as he'd been two months ago was a powerful one.

"Man, this one is killer," the boy said, opening the car door and sliding onto the leather seat. He gripped the oversize steering wheel, then ran his hand over the dashboard, inspecting the numerous gauges with awe. "Look at this," he said, pointing at a button on the floor next to his sneakered foot. "My dad says these old buttons on the floor are dimmer switches for the headlights."

"No," Erin said, "don't push it. That's the starter."

"No lie? Cool. A button instead of keys. You know a lot about these old cars, huh?" he asked, looking up with sudden admiration in his eyes.

"Well...no, not a lot." In fact, she knew next to nothing about cars from this era. So why had she known that button was the starter?

She was distracted by members of a tour group trailing out the open front doors of the mansion.

"Ostentatious, or what?"

"Naw. I think he had style. Knew how to live, if you ask me."

"Well, you can't convince me it was his partner who killed the wife. He did it, then bought off the police...."

Della. They were referring to her murder, Erin realized with sudden insight.

Della, I never meant to hurt you. Della, still so beautiful. J.B.'s words came back to her, and Erin was compelled to move up the steps toward the front doors. The inexplicable sense of déjà vu returned, this time even stronger, and she put a hand to her chest. Through the placket of her denim shirt, Erin felt the locket her mother had given her.

She frowned, feeling the odd sensation that she'd been here before—long before—intensify. Then her head began to swim, and, without warning, a vision burst into Erin's mind with such force and vibrancy that the exterior of the house seemed to vanish and her inner world became her only reality.

She found herself in a ballroom amid a crush of people. Loud, high-spirited jazz music competed with drunken laughter, and smoke swirled up from cigarettes held in long, jeweled holders. Chandeliers drizzled diamonds of light over revelers dressed in costumes from the roaring twenties, the same as the clothes she was wearing. In the center of the ballroom, couples moved with wild abandon to the jaunty rhythm of the music.

Seemingly from out of nowhere, a man appeared and stepped up to Erin's side. She caught her breath at the intensity of his stare. Did she know him? She'd never laid eyes on the man before, but there was a familiarity about him— No, it was more than that. They'd shared a past—confidences . . . secrets . . . intimacy. His look communicated that. And somehow she would have known it without the look, because she saw and felt more from this encounter than she had with any other man.

His black eyes, which were as dark as a winter night, narrowed, and a harsh scowl suddenly came over his handsome features. *What?* she felt compelled to ask. *What makes you so angry with me?*

His clothes were like the rest of the men's, indicating that he fit in with the others at the party, but somehow Erin knew this wasn't the case at all. He had a hard, rough quality about him that his fancy, civilized garb couldn't disguise. And it was that quality which had drawn her to him the very first time she'd seen him. First time? But this was the first. . . .

Chatter and giggles and raucous laughter spilled from the lips of the other partygoers, but his mouth was a grim, tight line. *Tell me!* she wanted to shout. *Why are you looking at me this way when I know you can't hate me? When I know you love me!*

The image broke apart as suddenly as it had formed, and the man's face seemed to disintegrate before Erin's eyes. She cried out at the profound sense of loss that overwhelmed her, gripping her heart, slicing at her soul. *No! Come back! Don't leave me.*

She came back to reality with a jolt. Her hand fell away from her chest and she stumbled back a step or two. As she stared at the front doors of the mansion, her mouth worked, but she couldn't speak . . . could barely breathe. Tears had gathered in her eyes.

Confused and shaken, she turned away from the doors, descended the steps and began running to her car. The gardeners, the people who had come to tour the mansion, the cars parked beneath the portico—everything and everyone became a blur at the edges of her vision as she bolted to the parking lot.

She fumbled at her car-door handle, her breath coming hard and fast, the man's face still devastatingly clear and real in her mind, and she dug in her pocket for her keys. Her heart pounded as she jerked the door open and slid quickly behind the wheel, then jammed the keys into the ignition. She swiped at the tears that had spilled from her eyes. Had it been a vision—or hallucination?—of a man she was certain she'd never met, yet also knew she loved...? Oh, God...

She could barely hear the engine of her car as it fired to life, so loud was the rushing of the blood in her ears. And still the man's face was there, his intense onyx eyes blazing, passionate.

She gulped in air, as she wrapped her hand around the gear shift. The mansion loomed in the rearview mirror, and Erin tried to look away, ordered her muscles to shift the damned car into reverse and her eyes to focus on the windshield. But she was unable to tear her gaze from the sight of the house, unable to escape what had just happened there and step back into reality.

The man was connected to the mansion in some way. And to her. That thought resounded in her head, and beat with the pulsing of her heart.

Connected... connected. She switched off the ignition with trembling fingers and turned around in the seat to look at the mansion again. Would there be answers inside?

"IT TOOK A FULL FIVE years to complete," Betty, the tour guide said. "Architects and artisans were brought in from all over the world to design and build it. Mr. Munro had expensive tastes and wanted the best of everything."

The guide pointed to the high ceiling, and Erin and the rest of the tour group glanced up. From her place at the back, she murmured in awe along with the rest of them. The entire ceiling was done in gold leaf!

The mansion fairly overflowed with one awe-inspiring feature after another. Erin's group had seen only half of the place so far, yet had already viewed the shiny chrome-laden kitchen that could easily have served hundreds of guests at once, beheld priceless paintings and sculptures and been allowed to run their hands over furniture that her mother would have killed for.

In his office had been a large portrait of J.B. His posture rigid and his expression dignified, he stood next to a chair where his first wife, Virginia, was seated, her hands folded in her lap. She was attractive, but had a stern mouth and no warmth in her eyes. And her husband was not the man in Erin's vision, as Erin had wondered before seeing the portrait.

She had searched each painting after that, hoping to find him, but hadn't seen him yet. She had also groped the entire time for an explanation for the strange vision, thinking that surely she must once have seen a picture of him, then buried his image in her subconscious. Maybe the *Munro Gazette* had run an article on the mansion's history with accompanying photos? Those first few weeks after his heart attack, her father had enjoyed listening to Erin read from the newspaper. It was possible, wasn't it, that she'd come across a photograph of the man there? But how could she have forgotten a face like his? How could any woman not remember the image of those sinfully black eyes, even if she'd seen them in a grainy newsprint photo?

Interrupting her thoughts, Betty—who'd been giving Erin the strangest looks—took them through a formal dining room paneled in rich mahogany. A huge stone fireplace with the Munro coat of arms on its mantel covered most of one wall, and several sets of china were displayed in lighted cabinets.

Next came the family's private quarters.

J.B.'s bedroom was the most impressive room in the mansion, definitely the lord of the manor's chamber. It was furnished in English baroque, Betty informed them, with chinoiserie side chairs, a massive walnut chest, and a huge bed inlaid with marquetry. Italian torchères lent circles of light to impressive Chinese vases.

The group then moved through various salons and parlors, a floor full of guest bedrooms, and even a handball court in the basement before finally reaching the last room on the tour.

"He had it fashioned after the great hall in a medieval castle that had been built by one of his ancestors," Betty informed them, sweeping her arm toward the oversize chairs and trestle tables. "This fireplace," she said, as she led them to it, "is amazing, isn't it?" She ducked her head, then stepped inside the huge brick enclosure, easily able to stand erect. "Notice the doorway back here? It leads to tunnels that J.B. had installed during construction of the mansion. Entrances have been found in other estate buildings such as the guesthouse."

"Oh, my. The tunnels... I'd heard about them," one of the women said excitedly. "Weren't they used to smuggle in bootleg whiskey during Prohibition?"

"Actually, no," Betty answered with a grin. "Remember, J. B. Munro founded the city. He served liquor at his parties and did little to conceal that fact. No, the tunnels were built more with convenience in mind. During construction of the house, the artists brought many of their treasures from the studio he'd built for them through the tunnels to prevent damage from the weather. After the mansion was finished, the tunnels were rarely used."

The woman frowned, apparently unwilling to have her romantic notions so quickly dispelled.

"But I heard that Pretty Boy Floyd once killed a man here over a poker game, then dragged the body out through the tunnels and dumped it in one of the lakes."

The guide shook her head. "Only a rumor. And if every rumor he's been linked to was true, he'd have had to be triplets."

"Can we see the tunnels? Go down inside them?" someone asked.

"I'm sorry." Betty pointed to the padlock on the door. "Closed by order of the fire marshal. But we do have one more item of interest on the tour. It was found just this week in one of the storage rooms of the tunnels. A portrait of J.B.'s second wife, Della."

Erin's stomach fluttered as she recalled that J.B. had called *her* Della. Her gaze followed the others' to the far end of the room where a very large portrait, covered with a black velvet drape, sat on a brass easel.

"His wife was murdered," the woman so fond of rumors declared as they all began walking in the direction of the portrait, Erin still in the rear. "I hear that the police thought J.B. did it."

"Actually," Betty continued with a note of impatience in her voice, "the murder was never solved. And J.B. was never listed in police records as a suspect. Again, that's merely a rumor. Their records show that Waite MacKinnon, Mr. Munro's partner in Munro MacKinnon Railway, was questioned. There was speculation about an involvement between him and Della Munro. He disappeared soon after her body was found in a cave here on the estate and was never heard from again."

"An affair! And then he disappeared after her murder? How did he kill her? I hear that—"

"She was strangled," Betty said curtly, her patience with the woman clearly spent. "Now, before we see the portrait, there's one other interesting thing about this great hall. Mr. Munro, a former Easterner, was intrigued with the history of his adopted state. He had a mural painted depicting that history. It's one of the most unique murals I've ever seen," she finished, then pointed to the ceiling.

Along with the others, Erin tilted her head up. There, covering the entire expanse of the room's enormous ceiling, was the painted history of Oklahoma. From the first settlers, to Indian Territory days, to the coming of the railroads, to recent governors, the mural had obviously been a lifetime project for J.B. The historical events weren't melded into one large collage, but were depicted in chronological rows so that anyone viewing it could see the order of what had happened.

"Now," Betty said when the group finally arrived at the portrait. "As I said, this is the last item on the tour so on behalf of all of us at the mansion, we'd like to thank you for coming. You're all welcome to stroll through the building at your leisure, or if you'd like to take the tour again, sign up in the office, please."

Betty then pulled back the drape. "Mrs. Della Richards Munro," she announced in a slightly theatrical voice, and stepped back for all to view the portrait.

Erin's eyes widened and her hand rose to her throat. "As you can see," she heard the guide say, "she's wearing the gown in the glass display case in her bedroom I showed you earlier. It's said she loved to have her picture taken and her portrait painted. She was quite attractive, wasn't she?"

The guide's words barely registered past Erin's shock, and moments later, when the group had dispersed, Erin hung back, rooted in place. She felt a hand on her shoulder and jumped.

"You kept to the rear of the group, but I couldn't help noticing," the tour guide said with a curious smile. She nodded at the portrait. "Are you... related somehow?"

"No," Erin managed to say. "No, I'm not."

Betty's forehead creased. "That's amazing. You're sure? Of course, we have no record of any living descendants, but the similarity is so striking—"

"No. I'm...not related. I promise you, I don't know these people at all." *Almost* not at all.

"How odd..." Betty began, then shrugged. "But you know what they say about everyone having a twin...."

"Yes, they do say that."

When she was gone, Erin stared at the portrait again, disbelief and confusion swirling in her mind. Odd? It might seem merely "odd" to Betty, but she didn't know about Erin's vision on the steps of the mansion, or about J.B. calling her Della and then knowing Erin's name when he had no way of knowing it. Now there was this portrait... This impossible portrait.

Shaking her head in denial, Erin noted Della's almond-shaped green eyes, her short auburn hair and heart-shaped face. *Impossible,* she thought again. This simply couldn't be Della Munro; Erin's mind simply refused to accept it.

Her complexion couldn't be that easy-to-sunburn impossible-to-tan shade of pink. Her jaw couldn't be slightly squared, and her chin couldn't have that small cleft in it. These simply couldn't be Della Richards Munro's features.

Because they were Erin's.

Della . . . Can you ever forgive me, Della? You're not Della. . . . You're the other one. . . . You're Erin. Erin closed her eyes, covering her mouth with a hand that trembled. Before she opened them, she prayed that her mind had been playing tricks on her and the image of Della Munro would be different. But it wasn't. In fact, the longer Erin stared at the woman, the more similarities she found. Their smiles were the same, both had noses that tipped up just a bit at the end.

Erin ran her hands through her own short-cropped auburn hair, then over her face, almost as though to assure herself that her features hadn't been stolen away to create this stranger's image.

She stepped closer to the portrait, within touching distance, and narrowed her gaze as she studied it more intently. It was then that her shock became complete; then that she noticed the locket.

It was just like the one—

She fumbled beneath the placket of her denim shirt and plucked hers out, tracing the etchings in the gold with her fingertips—the same designs as those on the locket that Della had worn for this portrait. Springing the latch, Erin wasn't that certain she would find nothing inside, even though it had been empty when her mother had given it to her.

To Erin's great relief, the locket was empty. On the heels of relief, she wondered exactly what it was she'd expected to find. An old photo of J.B.? One of the man Della was said to have had an affair with, Waite MacKinnon?

Or the man Erin had seen in her vision, the man whose image had compelled her to come inside.

She felt the same compulsion now. Stronger than the need to take her next breath, more tempting than vice to a sinner, it engulfed her and she watched in paralyzed amazement as, against her will, her hand reached for the portrait. At the same time the strange humming noise and the black cloud of foreboding she'd felt the day of Munro's death returned.

Erin grasped her own locket tighter—for what reason she didn't know—and when her fingertips finally made contact with the locket Della wore, she felt her hold on consciousness slip. Then blackness descended, like midnight blanketing a noonday sun.

CHAPTER THREE

WHEN SHE AWOKE IT WAS dark, cold and humid. The air smelled as though she was near a lake or ocean. But there was no movement, no sea breeze. The chill was dank and clammy. She lay flat on her back on a frigid, hard floor.

She tried to move, but found her limbs wouldn't cooperate. The only feeling in her arms and legs was a slight tingling sensation. She swallowed, fighting to will panic away. She could turn her head, and when she did, saw that she was in a hallway of some sort, about six feet wide by six feet high.

How had she come to be here? Where was "here"? And what had happened to cause her paralysis? The last thing she remembered before blacking out was touching the locket in the portrait.

Then came the sound of footsteps . . . voices. . . .

Erin glanced quickly to her left and saw two shadowy shapes, one large and one slight, walking in her direction from what seemed yards and yards away. A single naked bulb in a distant wall sconce provided little help. Erin squinted, but couldn't make out details like features, clothing and hair color. She could see nothing more than hazy silhouettes. She tried to call out, but like the rest of her body, her voice seemed to be afflicted with paralysis. Not even a whimper would issue from her lips.

Had she died...? Was this the famous tunnel leading to the light that those who had near-death experiences spoke of? But no. There was never pain or fear in the stories told by people who'd come so close to the gates of heaven. Their tales always included mention of being at peace, feeling secure and wrapped in warmth and love. Whereas Erin was most definitely afraid.

The pair continued moving toward her, then stopped about twenty feet away. She could see that the small figure was a woman, the larger one, a man—a man with a beard. Their features were still blurred, indistinct. She could hear their voices, and detected anger in the man's tone; fear in the woman's. But she couldn't make out their exact words.

Didn't they see her? They acted as though they were the only two people in this...this hallway. As if Erin weren't there.

Then the man turned his back to Erin, blocking her view of the woman, and their heated whispers quickly became exclamations, then angry shouts. She heard the sound of an open hand delivering a sharp, hard slap.

An all-out struggle began. Erin clenched her eyes shut and focused every ounce of her willpower on trying to move—anything; a finger, a toe. But her body had been leached of strength. Not a single muscle responded. She tried to shout again, but that was of no use, either. Her vocal chords were still frozen. Meanwhile the violence escalated rapidly, and Erin glanced back at the pair to see the woman's arms thrashing wildly. Her terror echoed from wall to wall.

Then there was silence. The woman's body slumped to the floor.

Erin turned her head away. A sob rose in her throat, but was trapped there. She felt tears slip from the corners of her eyes and stream into her ears. This couldn't be heaven. But, dear God, if it wasn't... what was it?

She heard footsteps again, and jerked her gaze back to the couple in time to see the man walking away from the body. He was leaving the way they had come in. Holding her breath, Erin watched until he was no longer visible, until the shadows had swallowed his image. The sound of a door opening, then scraping closed, echoed far along the hallway.

It was Erin's chance to help the woman. But how could she help when she couldn't move? God, what a nightmare. To have the skills but not the means to get close to the woman!

Just moments later, the nightmare intensified. Excruciating, fire-hot ribbons of pain snaked through Erin's body, and she gave an anguished cry. Starting in her shoulders, then traversing her torso, the wicked tendrils left searing agony in their wake. Had she been standing, the pain—unlike anything she'd ever known—would have driven her to her knees.

In her prone, paralyzed state, she could only grimace and suck in her breath as the pain spiraled down into her legs and radiated through her arms, stabbing every muscle, tendon and bone. Through clenched teeth, she hissed in a breath, then huffed it out in staccato bursts. Again and again. It was the only method at her disposal to fight the god-awful pain—the Lamaze breathing she'd learned in paramedic training.

Just as quickly as it had come, it was over, and Erin exhaled deeply. Tears of blessed relief filled her eyes. She lifted her hand to wipe them away, then almost shouted for joy. Her hand! She could move it again! And her feet, her legs…everything.

Adrenaline rocketing through her, she quickly sat up, and crawled to the woman's side, her locket bouncing against her chest.

"Oh, God!" she gasped, looking down at the woman's face. Nausea rose in her throat. It wasn't the angry red splotches that ringed the woman's throat like some sort of obscene necklace that brought on the urge to retch. Nor her vacant, open-eyed stare. Erin had seen death in many grisly forms. But none had been as revolting, as horrifying, as this. It was something she could never have imagined in her worst nightmare: she looked at the woman and saw her own face staring up at her.

"Oh, God," she whispered. "Della?"

No! Della had died before Erin was born! Sometime in the twenties, hadn't Chuck said? She swallowed convulsively, her mind numb as she checked for a pulse, a heartbeat, any sign of life. But there was none. She brushed her palm over Della's lids, closing the woman's eyes and swallowing again as her gaze took in the glamorous twenties-style gown and long strands of colored beads. Her feet were shod in elegant, T-strap heels, and her stockings were silk. She had the short, boyish haircut that had been in vogue in the twenties—not much different from the style Erin wore now. But her features— nose, mouth, eyes—were what riveted Erin's attention. Until she heard the door open again.

Footsteps echoed menacingly in the hallway.

The murder was never solved ... found her body in a cave on the estate. Erin remembered the tour guide's words and vaulted into action. Della's murderer had come back for the body. He was going to hide it in the cave. Though her mind should have reeled with the implications of that theory, Erin's survival instinct kicked in. She jumped to her feet and took off in the opposite direction.

ERIN SLID TO THE FLOOR and buried her head in her hands, wanting so much to give vent to tears of frustration and exhaustion. With every twist and turn of the hallway, with every new door she'd tried, she'd come no closer to finding her way out of the maze.

This had to be the system of tunnels J.B. had had excavated beneath the Munro mansion, but her mind refused to accept the rest of this "nightmare." That _couldn't_ have been Della Munro back there.

But what if it was? If she accepted where she was, and the woman's identity, wouldn't she have to accept _when_ she was? According to Della's date of death—

When she was? Oh, God. Erin squeezed her eyes shut. She'd lost her mind. She was actually entertaining the thought that she had traveled through time!

Rising from the floor, she decided to prove herself wrong. There had to be an explanation for how she had ended up here, for what she'd witnessed. And she would find it, by God.

Another half hour passed. She'd come to three more doors...three more *locked* doors. Exhausted now, her legs weak and trembling, she turned yet another corner and saw a set of concrete steps. At the top was a door.

Oh, please, she prayed, *let this be the one.* She urged herself on until finally she was grasping the metal railing, lifting legs that felt like they were moving in molasses. Halfway up, she stumbled and lost her footing, then fell down the hard steps. Her forehead connected with the concrete and she cried out in pain.

Her shins stung, and there would be bruises on her arms and torso. Checking her ribs, she was relieved to find none were cracked. Blood trickled from a goose egg that was swelling on her forehead.

She rose to her knees, then crawled up the stairs. Hope and desperation gave her the strength to stand, and she opened the door.

A blast of music assaulted her ears. What on earth? She moved through the doorway and glanced around her. An enclosure of bricks and mortar. Was she where she thought she was? The fireplace that Betty had stood inside? Ducking her head, she peered out into the great hall. The music came from a party that was in full swing; a party straight out of *The Great Gatsby*—and the one in her vision.

The men were dressed in suits with high, stiff collars, the women in satin and bugle-beaded gowns. A live band blared jazz from one corner, and blue-gray clouds of smoke from cigarettes and cigars drifted above the guests' heads.

"Della!"

Erin's gaze swung to the woman who had shouted. Decked out in a sleeveless satin gown and a long strand of pearls similar to the ones Della had been wearing, the woman handed her cocktail to the waiter standing next to her and rushed forward, the long feather in her glittery headband bobbing and a puzzled look in her eye.

"It *is* you, goose! Wherever have you been? For heaven's sake, we've wondered when you would— Oh, good Lord, you're bleeding!"

The woman grasped Erin's arm. "Come out of there," she said, staring at Erin's denim shirt and jeans in consternation. "What in heaven's name have you done to yourself?" She glanced back over her shoulder. "You," she instructed the waiter, who was gaping at Erin along with several nearby guests, "close your mouth and get J.B. over here!"

More heads turned. Conversations stopped. Several women edged forward, eyeing her clothing.

"She should probably sit...or something. Don't you think?" the woman asked the others, but no one answered. The waiter, dumbstruck, still hadn't moved. "What are you waiting for! Didn't I tell you to get J.B.?

"Really, dear," she commented, turning back to Erin once the servant had fled, "you might think about dismissing that one. Della, I'm not one to tell another woman how to run her household, but—"

Erin's head pounded. Her legs felt on the verge of collapse. She shook her head at the woman and dragged a shaky hand through her hair. "I'm... uh—" oh, this was just too bizarre! "—not who you think...."

Her words trailed off as the bevy of women surrounding her suddenly parted and a man elbowed his way through.

"J.B., there you are! Just look at Della! Ronald and I were wondering where she was—hadn't seen a trace of her since we arrived two hours ago—and I looked up and there she was in that monstrosity you call a fireplace, wearing these...these field hand's clothes! And look at the blood on—"

"Step aside, Leila."

His voice, sharp with anger, sliced through the woman's chatter. Her mouth snapped shut and she backed away quickly.

Erin blinked. God, it was really him! J.B. A younger, vital J.B. with thick, wavy blond hair and smooth, taut skin stretched over high cheekbones. The faded blue eyes that had once elicited her pity were now icy blue. And the scar! It was there, next to his eye. Amazing! What the devil was going on here? Was she dreaming? Was she hallucinating after that bump on her head? But no, that had been after she'd seen Della.... Oh, God.

J.B.'s hand encircled her upper arm none too gently, and he jerked up her chin with a forefinger. His eyes, hard with fury, examined the lump on her head. "Where the hell have you been?" he ground out. "And I'll have an explanation for these clothes!"

Explanation? Explanation! Her incredulity fled and anger streaked through her. Erin yanked her arm from his grasp. An explanation! *Yeah,* she thought sarcastically, *I could use one, too. Which line do I stand in for one of those!*

J.B. lifted a brow, momentary surprise in his gaze. Then his expression tightened and he reached for her arm again.

"She's hurt, J.B," a masculine voice intervened, and Erin glanced up. "You can see that."

"Oh, my God. It's you!"

Erin had never fainted in her life until today, but felt dangerously close to plunging into unconsciousness a second time. Her light-headedness burned off quickly, though, and her heart kicked with excitement. *I found you,* she almost said aloud. *You're... here!*

Oh, this was too unreal, she thought, examining his familiar features. They were just the same as they'd been in her vision. A lean, sun-weathered face, stubborn jaw, and eyes that were deep-set and pure black. Brows just as dark formed a vee at the bridge of his nose, and his eyes told her he was certain she'd lost her sanity. Hell, she probably had. No, not probably; of course, she had! Either that, or it was all a dream. One hell of a dream. She thought she saw a shift in his expression... imagined she saw a sharp glint of awareness in his eyes. She felt a surge of excitement at that and recalled the emotion she'd felt earlier, on the steps of the mansion. There was a connection here... something between them.

"Are you forgetting yourself, Waite?" J.B. demanded, jarring Erin out of her reverie. "She's *my* wife."

Waite? J.B.'s partner in Munro MacKinnon? The one Betty had said was rumored to have been Della's lover? The thought evoked sudden and inexplicable jealousy.

His jaw clenched. "Don't take that tone with me, J.B. When have I ever given you reason to distrust me?"

The moment was tight with tension, both men sending out masculine vibes, like two stallions taking each other's measure. Then J.B. seemed to remember Erin. He looked down at her. "You were forbidden to go down there. I'll hear your explanation later, after we've seen to your head. Let's go."

She was propelled forward by his hand at the small of her back, but not far, because she stiffened, instinctively bucking the order by digging in her heels. Erin didn't know what had happened to her, how she had ended up here—*when*ever the hell this was—but it wasn't in her nature to blindly follow commands. "No, I'm won't go anywhere with—"

"*No?* What is *wrong* with you?" His voice snapping with impatience, he swept his gaze over her jeans and denim shirt again before glancing at the guests who still hovered nearby. "I said now!" he muttered with more force.

"No! I—"

"You're hurt, Della." Waite stepped closer. His brow was furrowed, but his tone was soothing, persuasive. She watched, dazed as he lifted his hand toward her forehead, then winced when he grazed the bump. "See?" he said, lowering fingertips red with her blood into her line of vision. "You should go with J.B."

She swallowed, aware of the injury but more aware of the man who looked down at her, his expression urging her to obey J.B. *Can you take me?* she wanted to ask, but she realized that would only make matters worse.

Glancing away, breaking eye contact so she could concentrate, she made a decision. Yes, she thought, telling herself it wasn't his counsel she had decided to follow, but her own. She needed to think; figure out what had happened to her, and how she would get out of here, get home. Clearing her throat, she faced J.B. It felt strange, acting as though she were someone she wasn't, but Erin couldn't begin to fathom what might happen if she were to explain who she was... and what she had witnessed in the tunnel. "I...yes, J.B. Take me to...my room."

He wasn't pleased it had taken Waite's persuasion to convince her, it seemed, but he said nothing, merely nodded and led her through the crowd with brisk steps.

The great hall hadn't changed much, she noted distractedly. It was remarkably similar to the way it had looked on the tour. The walls were hung with priceless tapestries and canvases painted by world-renowned artists.

Then she saw the portrait and her footsteps faltered. She blinked, surprised again at the rendering of Della, astonished anew by the uncanny resemblance. Della, whose fate had been sealed by a man with a beard.

But even more surprising was the peculiar ringing in her ears that grew louder as she and J.B. approached the portrait. She almost wrote it off to her fall down the steps, then realized it wasn't a ringing noise at all.

It was humming. The same humming noise she had heard just before she had touched the portrait in her own world. Was this...a way back? Could it be that simple? she wondered, cautious hope stirring in her chest. But why not? If it was the "door" she'd entered to get here, logic said it was the door she would use to exit. With each step she took, the humming grew louder and her hope became stronger. As J.B. steered her toward the doorway beside the portrait, Erin broke away.

"What the—?" J.B. muttered disgustedly. He followed at her heels. "Della, you're testing me, woman." He reclaimed her arm just as she was reaching toward the canvas.

She shrugged out of his grip. "In a minute. Just give me one minute." But he frowned again, shaking his head and attempting to restrain her. "One minute or you'll have to drag me out of here, I promise you. Do you want that kind of scene?"

Erin seemed to have pushed the right button.

"All right," he said, teeth clenched. "One minute."

She didn't waste a moment. Lifting her hand to the portrait and sending up a short prayer, she closed her eyes and waited for the sensation of light-headedness. It didn't come. In fact, the humming ceased abruptly when her fingers made contact. She opened her eyes and saw that nothing had changed. Damn it!

Confused, Erin stepped back. Then the humming started again!

"Della, this is enough. I demand that you stop this...this whatever you're doing and come with me now."

She ignored him, intent on the portrait. Then she saw it and remembered. *The locket!* How could she have forgotten! She waved off J.B., fumbling inside her collar for the piece of jewelry. She hadn't just touched the portrait, she'd touched the locket at the same time. *It* was the key, she was sure of it, and—

Oh, dear God...the locket was gone. Gone? But she remembered having it on in the tunnel. Remembered it slapping against her chest as she'd crawled to Della's side. How could she have lost it between then and now?

"You've had your minute," J.B. said, breaking into her thoughts. "For God's sake, you're hurt."

She looked at him, then slowly lifted her fingers to the bump. "That's it," she whispered. "When I fell..."

Wheeling around, she made for the fireplace again.

"Della!"

But Erin didn't slow down. Not for J.B. or her exhaustion, not for the people in her way. Adrenaline and purpose sent her pushing and jostling, tripping and cursing her way through the crowd, until she was within yards of the fireplace. Yes! Her goal in sight, Erin elbowed past the last group of party guests, nearly sprinting the final few feet...only to be brought up short when Waite MacKinnon stepped into her path. She pitched straight into his arms.

"God." He grasped her upper arms, setting her back from him.

"Let me go," she said, short of breath. "I have to—go back down there—"

"Della!" He gave her a slight shake. "Are you drunk?"

"No! I'm not Della," she whispered heatedly, without thinking. "And I'm not drunk or sick! I just need to get back into the tunnel."

"You're going nowhere, Della, especially into that tunnel," J.B. said, rage painting his face in fiery splotches. He swung her around to face him. "You've finally done it, haven't you?" he stormed, clamping her arm in an inescapable hold, then dragging her through the crowd. "You've finally pushed me too far."

CHAPTER FOUR

STREAMS OF MORNING sunlight tickled the edge of Erin's slumber. As the bonds of sleep slowly unfurled, she heard whispered tones, female voices, coming from her radio. Snuggling deeper into the warmth of her bed, she fought waking. The most bizarre dreams had chased through her sleep all night, and now her head ached fiercely.

The morning disc jockeys' voices grew louder, and Erin shifted, pulling the pillow over her head. Becoming aware of dull aches in her arms and legs, she groaned. Strange. She'd done nothing out of the ordinary lately; in fact, these days she rarely did anything more strenuous than walk from one room to the next, fetching medication for Pop.

Pop! Erin sat up quickly, winced and clutched her head. Then she opened her eyes to the strangest sight.

Roses. Little pink roses and fussy trailing ribbons that decked the walls of her bedroom.

She blinked, then looked down at her lap. They were on her sheets, too. And the spread. She swept a hand across the fabric. These weren't her sheets and bedspread, nor did she recognize the wallpaper or retro furniture scattered about the room. Antique chairs and an old-fashioned floor lamp, a dressing screen with Art Deco panels. Everything in the room looked as though it had come from one of her mother's favorite antique shops.

She frowned, her gaze coming to rest on a wall next to the bed that formed an alcove of sorts, blocking out the rest of the room. Her head throbbing, and thick with grogginess, Erin lifted her fingertips to her temple and found a bandage on her forehead.

Bits and pieces of the crazy dreams from last night came at her. A maze... She had run through a maze and fallen down stone steps. She had stood inside a massive fireplace. People in funky 1920s costumes had danced through, and she remembered a teenage boy sitting in an antique car. Bizarre.

Hearing the women's voices again, she glanced around the room, searching for the radio. But there wasn't one. She scooted to the end of the bed, peering around the wall. Her eyes widened when she saw two women who stood next to an open closet. Dressed in black maid's uniforms, complete with white aprons and mobcaps, they were folding her jeans and shirt.

Erin looked down at the nightgown she wore, not remembering putting it on, not remembering ever buying one like it—not remembering anything. What was going on here? She squeezed her eyes shut, searching her fogged and pain-dulled brain for a clue.

"Shh!" she heard one of the maids say, her accent thick with Irish brogue. "Do you want her to hear you? She might be awake, you know!"

"Della Munro? Before lunch?" Erin heard the other woman's cynical laughter. "That, dear Annie O'Brien, I would love to see."

Della Munro.

Oh, God...Della Munro. The fog cleared and dread washed through Erin. Technicolor images, too real to be nighttime illusion, flared in her mind. She saw it all again, in crisp, sharp detail. She remembered the portrait, Della and the man who had strangled her, the party, J.B. and Waite, her lost locket. They hadn't been dreams, after all. But how—?

One of the maids turned slightly, and Erin ducked behind the wall.

"She has a good excuse for it today, I'm thinkin'. Have you forgotten that bump on her head?"

"And have you forgotten where she was when she got it, Annie? The tunnels. You know why she was in the tunnels. She was going to meet a—"

"Stop it, now! I told you I won't be listenin' to any more of the terrible things you say about the missus. I don't understand why you dislike her so. None of the other servants seem to. And she's a married woman, Edith, she wouldn't—"

"The others don't know what I know about her. And I'll tell you this, being married might mean something to folk like us, but not to the people who live in this palace. You're so green. Married, not married. Doesn't matter to them that have no morals. For pity's sake, you've heard the master half raised the girl before marrying her. These aren't decent, God-fearing people we're working for, Annie."

"Well, seein' with my own eyes will have to be believin' for me. She's been kind to me, Edith. She paid me while I was out sick for two weeks even though I'd only been workin' here less than six months. Not many would do that. And it's not my place to pass judgment."

"You think she was down in them tunnels just to while away the time? When her party was blaring away upstairs? She was meeting a man. Dressed up in men's clothes so she could sneak down there without drawing attention is my guess."

"I'll grant you the clothes are odd. But maybe...maybe she was dressed for riding? She does love that horse of hers. Maybe these are some kind of riding shoe. Saints, I've never seen the likes, and I thought those pointy-toed boots all the cowmen wear were strange.''

"Annie, you're worse than green, you're ignorant! She was with a man, which is what she loves more than horses, believe you me. Don't know where these shoes came from, never seen anything like 'em myself, either. But take a gander at this. Is that or is that not a *man's* name stitched on the side? Look here.... *Mike.*''

Erin frowned. Mike? On her shoes?

There was a moment's silence, then she heard Annie's soft giggle. "Oh, it's ignorant I am, is it? Well, I'm not so ignorant I can't spell a good Irish name like Mike. That's an *N*, not an *M*. It says Nike, you see. Heaven knows what it means, but it's not a man's name.''

Erin cracked a grin. *Nikee, Annie. It's Nikee.*

"Don't matter what it says on her shoes,'' Edith muttered defensively. "Matters what she was doing down in them tunnels. Might just get her sent away again.''

"Sent away again? No...I shouldn't hear about—''

"That's right. Same behavior got her thrown out of the castle four years ago. Oh, they tried to keep it as hushed up as possible, gave out the story that she was visiting family back east, but I heard the fight they had the night before she left. I know the real reason she was sent away. It was because of one of her affairs. He didn't want the whole town knowin' about it, even if she didn't care.''

Erin heard Annie sigh. ''Oh, Edith, you were listenin' at a door!''

''Couldn't help but hear it, Miss Greenhorn. They wasn't exactly whispering that night.'' There was a pause, then Edith's voice dropped. ''Sounded like he was going to beat her! He was hollering and slamming things down. And all she could do was cry and beg. Begged for him to let her stay in one breath, then wanted a divorce in the next!''

''Edith, I won't be listenin' to more of this.''

''Don't you even want to know the reason he was sending her off? The reason she wanted the divorce? It's a doozy. Yes sirree. The woman who's been so kind to you has quite the shameful secret in her past. She—''

The bedroom door swung open, and Edith's revelation was cut off in midsentence.

''Mr. Munro, sir!'' she exclaimed guiltily. ''We was just...just settin' Miz Della's clothes to rights. But we're finished. Let's go, Annie.''

More drawers were hurriedly slammed shut, and Erin heard the women scurry out the door.

She scooted back up under the covers, feigning sleep. This dream was turning into a nightmare!

How angry J.B. had been last night! And whether or not this was all some bizarre illusion, the pounding in her head was real. The last thing she needed right now was a fight.

The bed dipped when he sat on its edge. Erin felt his hand close over her shoulder, then shake her none too gently. "Wake up. Now, Della."

She kept her eyes shut, her features as still as possible. *Come on, give it up. Just go away.*

"I said now, Della." He shook her again. "You're awake and I know it."

Perceptive, Erin thought, but continued to breathe the rhythm of one folded deep in slumber. It was an effort not to move when she felt him come close, his face only inches from hers. That effort became gargantuan when his hand slid from her shoulder to her neck. Then his mouth was at her ear.

"Should I try waking you as a true husband might?" he whispered sarcastically. "One who actually shares his wife's bed?"

A fight *wasn't* the last thing she needed, she realized. Erin opened her eyes, glaring up at him.

He gave a bitter laugh. "Ah, I didn't think so," he said, then let go of her and stood.

He paced to the end of the bed and looked down at her. It startled her again, seeing the man's face. He was the man in the portrait she'd seen on the tour. But how? How could he be that same man? How could any of this be?

"What say we talk, wife." His tone was civil, and he wore a congenial grin, but his eyes were chips of stone. "About your hatred of me. About your quest to destroy my name in this town. Fascinating subject. Let's discuss it, shall we?"

Erin merely stared at him.

"No? Why, I was certain the subject would be of interest to you. Scandal and gossip being your forte, so to speak, I had supposed you'd be eager to talk about your latest efforts to disgrace me. Have you no comment at all on how you managed to fan the flames of rumor so vigorously just as they were dying down from four years ago? And at a party you so graciously offered to give in my honor! Surely you have something to say about that?"

Erin remained mute.

"Nothing? Wouldn't you like to gloat over how well your plan to humiliate me succeeded?" He dropped his facade of congeniality.

"You planned it so that several people saw you leave the great hall with that man, didn't you? And you're thrilled that everyone's talking about how you're at it again." His voice had risen in his anger, and Erin fought to prevent herself from wincing or covering her ears. "I ignored all the whispers and rumors these past months. More fool me for giving you and your compliant act the benefit of the doubt. You've been catting around again, just as everyone suspected. Everyone but *me!* And last night's scene was to show them, the people of my town, what a fool I've been, wasn't it?"

He ran a hand through his blond hair. His mouth was twisted in disgust and he jerked his gaze from her as though he couldn't stomach looking at her one moment longer. If this wasn't an illusion...if it turned out all this was real, Della, Erin thought, was some piece of work.

"Still nothing to say? Well, maybe this will stimulate some conversation," he said, his voice quiet again, but with menacing undertones. "You're obviously in need of some...*rest,* dear. A good deal of it. So I placed a call early this morning to a hospital in Missouri."

Rest? Hospital? "Wh-what do you mean?" She broke her silence warily. This was feeling more real by the moment. And more frightening.

"Ah, I thought that might make you speak up. What I mean is that though it usually takes a little while for the commitment papers to go through, I seem to have enough of a name left to...expedite matters. And your actions last night can only help."

Commitment! Erin sat up straight in the bed, her mind filling with images of—what had they called them in the 1920s?—asylums. Before reform had come about. Oh, no. No way. She might have suspected she'd lost her mind a time or two since last night, but she hadn't. Deep down she knew she was sane. It was her circumstances that were crazy. But that didn't mean she was going to let them get more crazy. She knew how to extract herself from the situation: the portrait; and the locket.

Time for the truth, she thought. Time to tell him she wasn't the woman he planned to put away. She wasn't his adulterous, scandal-mongering wife, Della. That woman was dead and hidden in some cave around here, and Erin was a paramedic who had treated him in the 1990s and—

Oh, God, that really *did* sound crazy. It was impossible. Unbelievable. And just what he needed for the commitment papers!

No, she couldn't tell him the truth—not without Della's body as proof. And finding Della could take…who knew how long? Weeks, maybe. She'd bet J.B.'s timetable wouldn't allow for weeks. Her best bet was to avoid the truth at all costs and get the locket back!

Erin swallowed, fighting panic. *Think. Think. You only need to stall him, then you're out of here.*

"Still nothing to say, Della?" He folded his arms across his chest, a cocky, satisfied grin on his face. "I'm so pleased to see you agree with my plans. Though, whether you feel it's the rest you need or just that you're bored with the local crop of young men, I don't know. Nor do I care. In fact, it does my heart good to see you floundering for once.''

Oooh, Erin thought, angry now. She was furious about the whole mess she found herself in—incensed about feeling even momentarily helpless, and particularly enraged by *him*. Della might have been the biggest slut in the history of the Sooner State, but her husband was no saint, either. This wasn't the frail old man she'd met as a paramedic. He wasn't weak or pitiable—he was dangerous!

She watched his eyes, bright and cold with a devious light, and knew that nothing short of feeding him a dose of his own medicine would get her out of this predicament. She cleared her throat and leaned her head back against Della's ornate headboard. Summoning up a bored expression, she said, ''You underestimate me, you know. And that surprises me. You haven't risen to the place you are by underestimating people.''

Not a flicker of emotion showed in his features, and Erin felt a prickle of nerves. Could she pull this off?

''You're right. I underestimate no one. I will admit to weakness in the past where you're concerned, but I've learned from my mistakes.''

Erin smoothed the bedcovers with a hand she ordered not to shake. ''I wouldn't be too quick to put my John Hancock on any dotted line if I were you. Not if you want the little 'episode' of four years ago to remain a deep, dark family secret. Wouldn't want the whole of Munro society to get wind of it, would you?''

He laughed then, shaking Erin's confidence. Hadn't Edith told Annie that J.B. had wanted whatever had happened hushed up? Erin had so hoped she'd found J.B.'s Achilles' heel.

''Blackmail? Aren't you forgetting that adultery is your forte?'' His laughter died a quick death. ''Mark my words. If you try anything with me, Della, I'll see to it that you're locked away in that hospital until everyone in this town forgets you ever existed.''

He'd made his threat sound convincing, but Erin noticed something. J. B. Munro had a tic. A nervous tic beneath one eye. *Not quite as unnerved as you'd like me to believe, are you?* she thought.

''But what about the damage I'd do to the precious Munro name before the key's turned in the lock?''

''Munro happens to be your name, as well.'' The tic became more noticeable. He rubbed at it with his index finger, then caught her watching and shoved his hands into his trouser pockets.

''One would think by my behavior that I don't particularly care about the Munro name,'' she said with a shrug. Inside, she cared. Oh, how she cared—but not for the Munro name. So much was riding on her ability to pull this off. What if threatening to tell family secrets wasn't enough? It might be pushing her little scheme too far, but Erin decided she had to take the bluff one step further.

"I don't underestimate people, either, J.B. I knew you'd threaten something like this after I slipped out last night. So I've made sure you'd pay for it if you did." She took a deep breath. "That man everyone saw me leave with? He knows all the details you tried to keep hushed up four years ago. He's known for quite a while, in fact. If it gets out that I've decided to 'visit family back east' or something like that, I've told him to make sure the details get out."

J.B.'s eyes widened almost imperceptibly. Erin's pulse quickened. "He . . . has a relative who's a reporter," she added for good measure.

"A relative?"

"His cousin."

"Local paper?"

"National."

"I don't believe you."

"Your choice."

He balled his hands into fists. The tic worked furiously. "You're not stupid, Della. You know you're crossing the wrong man," he said with a growl.

"Am I?" she asked, lifting a brow. "Well, J.B., I see it differently. The way I see it is that *you're* crossing the wrong *woman*."

"That woman is my wife," he spat out, but he might just as well have used the word *property*.

"And this wife will not spend one day, one minute, in any hospital. Not if her husband cares about his precious name."

It became a glaring contest then. J.B. was a pro, she'd give him that. Arms folded across his middle, his neck and face a blotchy crimson color above the high, tight collar, he spewed contempt from his narrowed eyes.

As determined as J.B. was, however, he was the one to break eye contact first. He shook his head, and his hands went back into his pockets. For one brief moment Erin detected sadness in his eyes. But it was swiftly gone, probably only a figment of her imagination.

"You may feel you've won at the moment," he said quietly, his features suddenly carved with the determination she was sure had been the driving force behind all the millions he'd made. "But the victory might not be quite as sweet as it tastes now." He stalked toward the door, and Erin let out a silent breath of relief, glad for the wall that blocked the bed from his view. She listened intently to his fading footsteps, waited for the sound of the door opening.

"You are restricted to the mansion," he said from across the room. "You will not venture down into those tunnels, or do anything else to embarrass me in front of Harrison Wyndham while he's staying here. This town has too much invested in his cooperation, and I won't see you destroy what I'm trying to do. You want to stay here, you'll play the role of adoring wife if it kills you. And it just might."

The door closed and Erin fell forward on the bed, face first into the rose-and-ribbon-patterned bedspread, muffling her load groan.

The tension of moments ago might have lessened with J.B.'s departure, but the fear hadn't— fear that she might have pushed the powerful man too far. She was out of her league here; way, way out of it.

Which meant she had to get moving. Throwing back the bedclothes, she got to her feet and went to the dresser she had seen Edith and Annie standing beside. Her head still throbbed as she searched for and found her Levi's. She had them over her hips and buttoned when she chanced to look out the tall, leaded windows above the dresser.

Too much, she thought. *Too much!* The room overlooked the front of the mansion, offering a view of the circular drive before it disappeared under the portico. Lining the drive were maybe a dozen or more cars similar to the ones she'd seen the day of the tour. Yesterday, she thought. But in reality, seventy years from now. And those cars— she remembered model names like Lexington, Maxwell, Pierce-Arrow—were likely only a few years old, if that. Yesterday they had been antiques.

She saw people stream out the front doors and cluster around the cars. Munro's party guests had obviously stayed overnight. Erin pressed closer to the windows, her eyes widening as she took in their apparel. Had she not been seeing it all in vivid color, she would swear she was watching an old black-and-white movie. She could almost hear the scratchy old sound track as guests gathered outside.

Women in cloche hats and coats with high fur collars were escorted out on the arms of men in stiff collars like J.B.'s, and wearing black bowler hats and overcoats. She caught sight of a younger man who didn't wear a hat, but certainly should have, in her opinion. His hair was as shiny as patent leather, slicked back and parted in the middle.

She glanced down at her jeans, knowing she would be sure to stand out—something she didn't want. Taking only a moment to mourn their loss, she went to Della's closet and flung the door open.

The tour guide hadn't exaggerated. Della Munro had been a slave to the fashions of the day. Erin clattered hanger after hanger of designer outfits across a metal bar, her amazement growing with each label she read. Worth, Chanel, Vionnet, Lanvin, Patou. Nothing like conspicuous consumption, she thought, brushing her fingertips over the satiny fabric of an Egyptian-looking silver evening gown. She might have been a piece of work, but Della Munro knew how to live large.

Erin chose the plainest of Della's daytime outfits, then moved back to the dresser to stow away the jeans. The change in her pocket jingled. Pulling out her money and license, she focused on the birth line of the small card: 1966.

She looked skyward, her stomach roiling with the impossibility of it all. "I'm not due here for another forty years. You realized that, didn't you?"

CHAPTER FIVE

ERIN CAME TO A HALT on the landing. The foyer of Munro's magnificent home sprawled out below her, shafts of sunlight streaking through the fanlight above the giant wooden front doors. Alabaster sculptures on pedestals flanked the entranceway, and the spectacular Italian marble floor gleamed like a winter pond in moonlight.

She closed her eyes and moaned quietly, wishing she had paid more attention when she'd taken the tour. The great hall was at the back of the mansion on the first floor, that much she remembered. This, of course, was the front. She had just spent twenty minutes fighting her way through the labyrinth of the upper floors, taking turn after wrong turn into bedrooms, sitting rooms and parlors, even managing to stumble into J.B.'s office. He'd glared at her from behind his desk and she'd backed out of the room, whispering a huffy, "Excuse me," under her breath while making her escape.

Escape. That's where she'd prayed this staircase would lead. She had envisioned leaping off the last step into the great hall, then breaking Olympic records in her dash toward the fireplace and the door that would take her to her locket, then home to her father's bedside. Now she stood on the landing, eyeing an arched door that led to the dining room, the distinct aroma of breakfast wafting up the stairs to tempt her. Her stomach growled as if on cue.

"Tough," she told it, then proceeded down the stairs as quietly as she could in Della's uncomfortable high heels.

She slipped past the dining-room door, hoping no one had noticed her, then quickened her steps. If memory served, there were only a couple of football-stadium-size rooms between her and her goal.

She fairly flew through the first room, attracting no attention because, thank heavens, it was empty. But as she strode briskly through the next one, a maid looked up from an armoire she was dusting. The woman opened her mouth as though to speak, but Erin flashed her a "You don't want to mess with me right now" look. The maid promptly closed her mouth and averted her eyes, then continued with her dusting.

When Erin finally entered the great hall, she paused for a moment to make sure it was empty. It was. Thank God. Just steps away from freedom.

More like yards, actually. This room was the showcase of J.B.'s palace—the tour guide had said so herself. Larger than any other in the mansion, the room had space enough to hold three gala balls at once. Erin thought of the music from last night as she passed the bandstand where the baby-grand piano stood silent now. She thought of the crowd of twenties flappers and their slick-haired companions as she tip-tapped across the expanse of black-and-white tile.

When she finally stood in front of the king-size medieval fireplace, she thought of J.B. and Waite.

Waite. Erin paused, her hand on the brick facade. She thought she felt his presence, and turned, expecting to find him there. He wasn't. But he should have been, because her throat had filled again with the same fierce emotion she'd felt last night.

There was no sense to be made of it, of course, but Erin found it strange how passionate her feeling for Waite was. Oh, hell. She rolled her eyes. Reason? She was looking for reason? Nothing that had happened here made sense. The connection was the portrait, though, and Della's murder. Not Waite.

She ducked and walked into the shadowy fireplace. Stepping to the back, she wrapped her fingers around the doorknob and twisted. Then pulled. And pulled again. The knob turned easily, but still the door wouldn't give. Glancing up, she saw why. A padlock was threaded through a hasp at the top of the door.

"Damn you, J.B.!" Erin grabbed the lock, banging it against the door again and again as though that actually might do some good. "Damn you, damn you, damn you!"

"Having trouble?"

Erin gasped, then swung around, expecting to see J.B. But it wasn't him. It was Waite. He stood at the opening of the fireplace, hands on hips, his head lowered to peer in at her. Her nerves, already frayed, exploded when he stepped into the enclosure.

"Uh...yes. Actually, I could use your help." Attraction, she told herself, backing up against the door. That's all it was. He was her fantasy type: tall and dark, with mystery in his eyes and a mouth that made her think of...well, sex. She'd never been quite this blindsided by attraction in the past, but Erin was no innocent. She knew chemistry when she felt it. And that's all this was. Nothing mystical about it.

"Could you, now?"

The second dose of sarcasm stung a bit. "Yes. As I told you last night, I need to get into the tunnel."

Even in the dim light she could see that his complexion was ruddy, as though he'd just stepped in from the cold, and the scent of outdoors clung to the clothes that fit his strong body so beautifully.

He stared down at her, lifting a gloved hand to his mouth, and clasping one of the fingers in his teeth and pulling it off. Then he looked up at the padlock, fingering it. A flutter of sexual awareness settled in Erin's stomach. *See?* she told herself. *Sexual attraction, pure and simple.* She glanced up at his hand. It didn't surprise her for some reason that his was callused, used to physical labor. But should it be? He was a tycoon, and tycoons sat behind desks.

Finally she found her voice. "You see, I lost something down there. A piece of jewelry. And I want to get it back."

"And you'd like me to help you open this lock so you can go down there."

"Yes. That is—do you mind?" She made the mistake of looking up at him, her gaze meshing with his. It struck her that Della would have been crazy *not* to have been tempted by a man like Waite MacKinnon. Not that Erin condoned the woman's loose interpretation of her marriage vows, but she had been human. And so was Erin.

Human and female and inexorably drawn to everything about this man. Good Lord, she could think of nothing at the moment but touching him. She tucked her hands behind her back.

"Do I mind?" The indolent smile on his mouth was crooked, and a dimple slashed one cheek. "Looks like J.B. might mind. It appears as though he doesn't want you down there."

"I realize that," she replied, an edge to her words as she recalled J.B.'s dictatorial stance. "But he doesn't have to know, does he?"

Waite narrowed his eyes. The dimple vanished. "*He doesn't have to know*, Della? Is that what you told the man you took into the tunnels last night?"

The sharp tone in his voice made her blink. It seemed Waite cared a little more about Della's behavior than was appropriate. Was that part of the legend correct, then? Was Waite more than just a friend to Della? She remembered him telling J.B. something about not having reason to distrust him. But maybe he'd lied. Waite wasn't Della's murderer, but maybe the rumors of their affair hadn't been just rumors.

"I don't want to talk about last night," she said. Because, of course, she didn't know enough about last night to discuss it. All she was aware of was that Della was dead, and at the hands of a bearded man who very well might have been the one who'd done the luring. But Erin had neither the time nor the inclination to come to Della's defense. "I just want my locket back, okay? Can you help me or not?"

"Your *what?*" Waite's features froze, surprising Erin.

"My...locket."

"Had a change of heart, have you?" he asked.

"I don't know what you're talking about."

He gave a short, humorless laugh. "You know exactly what I'm talking about."

No, Erin thought wearily, *I really, really don't.* Trying a different tack, she reached up to the bandage on her forehead. "I'm, uh, not thinking clearly today. I can't remember. I think this bump on my head—"

"You gave it away," he interrupted. "To a maid, remember? Told me you hated it." A smirk hitched one corner of his mouth. "It *and* me."

Waite pushed his hand back into his glove, surprised at Della's stunned expression. Her fingers dropped from the bandage and her mouth worked, but no words came out. Della Munro at a loss for words—an even bigger surprise.

"So...*you* gave her the locket?"

He frowned. "Her?"

"Me. I—I mean me," she said quickly.

"You can't tell me you don't remember that. Della?" He took her chin in his hand and forced her to look up at him.

"I... well, of course I remember it. It's just that..."

"Just what?"

"It's just... my head. I'm not feeling well. You know, I should probably go lie down or something." She edged her chin away from him and her hand shot to the bandage again. "Yeah, that's what I need to do. I'll, uh... I'll catch you later. I mean *see. See* you after a while," she amended, then fled the fireplace.

Waite ducked down, watching as she strode briskly from the room. When she was out of sight, he stepped out of the fireplace and rubbed a hand over his face. He'd vowed a good long while ago to put J.B.'s wife out of his thoughts completely, and he'd been damned successful at it for years. So what had happened over the past twenty-four hours to change all that?

Last night she'd looked at him, and touched him, and he'd been rocked back on his heels. And just now, when he'd pictured her going down to the tunnels with that man, he'd experienced an impossible swell of jealousy that hadn't been there when he'd actually seen her leave with him in the first place.

He clenched his teeth. This was stupid. After cleansing his mind and his soul of the woman, he wasn't about to crawl back into the mud with her.

She wasn't worth a moment's consideration. And certainly not worth the restless hours he'd spent last night.

I'll catch *you later?* What the devil did that mean?

He'd been skeptical when she'd blamed the injury to her head for her strange behavior, but thinking back to the party and then her recent actions, he wasn't so sure she hadn't been telling the truth.

I'm not Della.

He'd suspected liquor last night, rum being Della's favorite beverage these days. What else could have explained her disjointed ramblings and the clothes she wouldn't be caught dead in?

His gaze was drawn to the portrait J.B. had commissioned when she'd been his ward, not yet his wife. Waite wandered slowly toward it. He stood before it, looking at the young girl who had possessed his love and all his dreams for the future, and the years melted away.

He heard gay laughter trill from her lips, then felt her kiss him, remembering the passionate response only a young man in the throes of first love could know. He saw the heat of arousal in her heavy-lidded eyes, eyes that had gazed upon him with what he'd mistaken for love. He felt the caress of her elegant hand on his skin, the slide of their bodies when joined in the age-old rhythm of lovemaking. And he heard the music their whispers and groans had made when sweet release had finally come.

"Beautiful woman, J.B.'s wife."

Waite started, turning. Harrison Wyndham, the Boston banker who was J.B.'s houseguest, stood behind him, his head tilted as he studied Della's portrait with a curious expression. Waite hadn't heard his approach. He cleared his throat, then his mind, of the images. Good God, those days—their days—had been a lifetime ago. And he'd thought the memories had gone the way of his innocence . . . his youth.

"Yes," he replied. "She is."

"But a bit . . . wild, eh? Quite a spectacle she made of herself at the party."

Waite tensed, and felt a twist of irritation toward the banker. He didn't like the look in Wyndham's eye, or his judgmental attitude. True, Waite had engineered the deal between J.B. and Wyndham, but that didn't mean he had to like his attitude toward Della.

Della . . . his partner's wife. That, Waite told himself, was what had made him feel so protective. But when he searched for a judicious retort, it was difficult to find a defense for her behavior. He, himself, had thought her drunk.

"High-spirited," Waite said at last. Wyndham squinted behind his small, round spectacles.

"High-spirited, wild. I suppose Oklahomans see no distinction between the two. Not with your horses or your women."

Sudden ire was supplanted by a prick of discomfort. Della wasn't his woman. Not anymore. Waite shouldn't feel this unreasonable need to defend her. She had J.B. for that. But still the words rankled. He said with a grin that didn't reach his eyes, "Even here on the 'uncivilized' prairie, Wyndham, we know the subtle distinction."

"Subtle?" The banker chuckled and slid his hands into the pockets of his elegantly cut trousers. His gaze swept the great hall and all the trappings of J.B.'s success, coming back to rest on Waite. "Mr. MacKinnon, don't take this as an insult, because I'm a businessman, and this display, ostentatious though it might be, speaks to me of accomplishment. But I must say I find it amusing to hear the word *subtle* on the lips of an Oklahoman. In the East, Munro's wife's behavior last night would not have been referred to as 'high-spirited' any more than it would be said that J. B. Munro lives 'comfortably.' "

Waite fought back his anger. He and J.B. had spent an entire year convincing Wyndham to visit. He was president of a bank in Boston that boasted some of the wealthiest, old-monied clients on the Eastern seaboard. J.B. wanted a good portion of that money to be invested in Oklahoma, and in Munro specifically.

Waite wasn't entirely in agreement that Munro needed Wyndham's clients and their fat wallets, but he'd played his part nevertheless. Still, prosperity was already theirs. When other rail lines like Munro MacKinnon had been forced out of business by the gasoline age, Waite had suggested diversification, and J.B. had been in complete accord. Investing in everything from oil to holdings in trucking lines, city buses, and even radio manufacturing, they had then poured private funds into civic improvements such as the paving of all city roads and the building of a hospital, a city pool and a golf course. The citizens of Munro enjoyed a healthy economy. J.B. argued that it wasn't enough; his town needed more.

Waite wondered fleetingly when J.B. would ever have enough. For himself or the town.

"On Oklahoma's behalf," he said, avoiding mention of Della, "I'll take it as a compliment, Harrison. I was born in the East myself, but I became accustomed to the grand scale of things here quickly. We feel if you don't do it up big, it must not have been worth doing in the first place."

Wyndham snorted. "It must have taken some getting used to, you being from the East. Don't know that I could ever become acclimated to a place like this."

Waite shrugged, annoyed by the banker's attitude, but relieved that the conversation had veered into safer territory. Safer for J.B.'s business concerns and safer for Waite's personal peace of mind. *Peace of mind...* He wouldn't, couldn't let thoughts of Della Munro creep back in again.

"I was a boy when I arrived, Harrison. Probably didn't have the sense to be intimidated." His grin was self-deprecating. "Like most young men, it was the adventure, the romance I'd heard stories of, that appealed to me."

A frown puckered the banker's brow. "My clients, normally serious, no-nonsense men, are quite taken with the glamour of the West. I'm afraid that might bias their good business sense. But I'm not so easily impressed."

Waite held back a wry grin. "No romance in your soul, Harrison? I find that hard to believe."

"No room for it in business, Mr. MacKinnon." Wyndham grasped the lapels of his jacket, reminding Waite of every stuffy, pragmatic banker he'd ever met. "Didn't get where I am today by allowing emotion to color the facts in a business transaction. Oklahoma, in my opinion, is merely another state amongst many my clients might wish to locate their business interests in. No more or less glamorous than any other.''

''Then I suppose a trip to the 101 Ranch to see the Wild West show J.B. had planned for you would be out of the question.''

''Wild West show, you say?'' Then, quick to stifle his sudden interest, the man harrumphed. ''Seen plenty of them. One in Madison Square Garden.''

''Ah. Well, the 101 is the best of the lot—world renowned, in fact. But since you don't seem interested...''

Wyndham's eyes shifted nervously behind his spectacles. ''Oh, but I wouldn't want J.B. to change his plans for me. No, I'll go along. Probably be best for me to meet the owner of this concern. He's another businessman, after all.''

''Yes, one of the more successful ones in Oklahoma.''

''Then I shall attend. No need to tell J.B. he should cancel his plans.''

''Oh, I wouldn't think of it, Harrison.''

''Good, good. Well, good morning to you, MacKinnon. I'm heading in for breakfast, myself.''

''Enjoy,'' Waite said, his lips quirking when the banker left the room. Wyndham made one poor poker player, Waite thought, having witnessed the man tip his hand all week. He could bluster on about his pragmatism from hell to breakfast, but the man was a goner. Had been since he'd stepped out of J.B.'s private railroad car and laid eyes on his first cowboy.

Congratulations, J.B. That meant more prosperity. More money. Which, of course, meant more wealth for Waite. He couldn't say why, but the prospect brought him little satisfaction. Suddenly other things seemed far more important—such as his inappropriate thoughts about his partner's wife.

He should be glad that the deal was going to go through. He was going to need the money. Soon he'd be moving into the lavish home that was nearly finished, the mansion he'd vowed to have the first time he'd stepped through the doors of J.B.'s palace. *One day,* he had thought, *I'll have all this.* And that day was finally here. But it had brought none of the pleasure or excitement he'd once anticipated.

Touring the cavernous, empty rooms of his new residence yesterday, he'd only felt a niggling sense of irritation. It was too big, too...much. It wasn't as he'd imagined it would be at all. The floor plans he'd approved hadn't included such ridiculously immense rooms—had they? And had he told the builder he'd wanted so many bedrooms? Foolish to have that many bedrooms. He didn't entertain out-of-town guests, and he didn't envision ever having a family of his own.

And why the hell not? a small voice in the back of his brain asked. *You could still do something about it, could have married years ago.*

He glanced up at the portrait again, then damned himself—and her. Della Munro had not been the woman for him eight years ago, and no way in hell was she the right woman now. So why had he looked at her portrait when he'd thought of filling his huge new house with a family? She was J.B.'s. He'd accepted that; he hadn't thought twice about her after finally realizing that his partner had done him a favor by taking her for his wife. Until now. Now?

With teeth clenched, Waite forced himself to remember. If anything would put an end to this nonsense, refreshing his memories of Della ought to.

Della had been seventeen, just days from her eighteenth birthday, when he first saw her. Waite had been twenty-two, fresh out of college and a new employee of Munro Rail Lines. He'd taken one look at Munro's ward and fallen hard. Head-over-heels, knocked-on-his-keister hard. At Della's insistence, they met on the sly, and before long she'd given him every reason to think she felt the same way about him. Waite had wanted marriage, a family to take the place of the one he'd lost, and he'd proposed. It had seemed strange at the time, the shrewd grin that had stretched her lips. But it had made sense later, of course, when J.B. informed him a marriage between Waite and Della would never happen—because J.B. planned to wed her himself.

Though Waite had exploded with fury at the time, Della's coldhearted rejection after J.B.'s announcement had convinced Waite that she'd never really loved him, had only used him for her own purposes. She had had her sights set on J.B. all along, she'd informed Waite flippantly, and their affair had simply been a means to an end. She had wanted J.B.'s attention, and what better way to get it than through a dalliance with Waite, J.B.'s favorite young "lieutenant."

He had nursed a bruised heart and a battered pride for a long time, but he'd gotten over her. He and J.B. had made peace, as well, and over time the whole sordid episode faded into memory.

Until now, the small voice reminded him.

Yes, Waite thought. Until now.

He glared at the portrait, suspicion displacing the indifference he'd felt toward Della all these years. *You're up to something again, aren't you?* he thought, and chastised himself for forgetting even for a moment that Della did nothing without an ulterior motive. Why else would she solicit his help in finding the locket?

Waite turned away from the portrait, deciding he'd have no part in whatever Della was cooking up. He frowned, remembering his living arrangements for the time being. Until his new home was finished, he'd accepted J.B.'s invitation to stay in the Munro guesthouse. That was far too close for comfort. But then, where Della was concerned, there wasn't enough distance between here and China.

CHAPTER SIX

ERIN RACED UP THE STAIRS, looking back over her shoulder, half expecting all the hounds of hell to be nipping at Della's shiny black heels. In reality, it was only one particular hound she was worried about.

Waite MacKinnon.

She dashed through the second-floor hallway, taking a turn here, a turn there, trying her damnedest to find her way back to Della's bedroom. She didn't know why, exactly. She should be looking for an ax to break down the door to the tunnel, but all Erin could think of was putting a thousand miles between herself and Waite.

So *Waite* had given Della the locket. Waite, the gorgeous railroad magnate, and Della, the wife of his business partner, *were* intimately involved. Erin's face flooded with heat at the thought. Good Lord, she *was* Della now. For all intents and purposes, and for however long it took to get out of here, she was stuck living Della's life. Waite had seemed angry with her in the fireplace; in fact everyone she'd met in this decade seemed to feel that way toward Della. But there was no telling when Waite's anger might fade, and then what? And what about J.B.? What if he decided to demand his marital "rights"? It didn't bear thinking about.

For heaven's sake, she thought, glancing upward. *I needed a life, okay? I'll admit it—I was definitely life-challenged for a while. But come on, isn't this a bit too much?*

But it wasn't intimacy with J.B. that filled her thoughts. It was the picture of Waite that dominated her mind, and she felt the heat leave her face and make a molten journey through her body. She saw them together in all manner of places, all manner of positions, his hands caressing her, hers clutching his strong shoulders. She heard their mingled sighs and groans, felt his mouth on her skin, and hers on his—

"Oh! Have a care, missus!"

Annie's warning came too late, and Erin, her mind deep in fantasy, collided with the poor maid as she exited a bedroom, her arms loaded down with boxes. Annie fell hard on her backside, her cargo pitching hither and yon. Had she been wearing her Nikes, Erin probably wouldn't have lost her balance, but no amount of arm waving could save her from landing squarely on her posterior, as well.

"Oh, missus!" Annie crawled quickly to Erin's side. "Are you all right, missus? I'm that sorry, I am!"

"It wasn't your fault, Annie. It was an accident."

"But had I warned you quicker it might not have happened. And you with your head already injured! I had my thoughts in the clouds as usual," she said with a groan.

Erin chuckled and stood, helping Annie up. "Believe me, you weren't the only one whose thoughts were elsewhere." Warmth flooded her cheeks when she remembered just where *her* mind had been.

Annie began restacking the boxes.

"Let me help," Erin said, and picked up the two closest to her.

"No, missus. You just sit still." The maid snatched the boxes from Erin's hands and then, in a flurry of movement, had them restacked in a wink. She stood, lifting her burden.

Erin got to her feet, frowning. Annie was slight of stature, and the armful she carried was obviously too heavy. "Here, let me have some of those."

Annie gave her a curious look. "It's me job, missus."

"But I don't mind help—"

"Oh, I wouldn't hear of it. And you'll pardon my sayin' so, but should you be up and around, dashin' about the halls so soon after hurtin' your head?"

"Oh, no, I'm fine now," Erin said, and took two boxes off Annie's stack. "Where to?"

The maid's brow creased and she sighed. "This way, then." And she struck off down the hall, mumbling under her breath.

"Oh, come on, Annie. I'm not an invalid," Erin said, right behind her.

Annie shot a glance over her shoulder. "Well, it's none of my business, of course, but you coulda stood another day's bed rest. As me ma will tell you, your health's all you have, you know."

"A wise woman, your mother."

Annie opened a bedroom door and led the way in. She set down her boxes next to a closet. Erin placed hers on top of them. "Oh, she's that, and don't you forget it. She'd be advisin' you against the party tonight."

Annie opened the closet door, grabbed a box and rose up on tiptoe to put it on a shelf. Erin, taller than the petite maid by several inches, grasped her by the shoulders and switched places. "You hand them to me, I'll put them on the shelf."

Annie's brow puckered and her jaw set. Erin chuckled. "Oh, stop worrying. You were telling me about your mother."

Annie handed her a box. "Yes, and I'll tell you this. You wouldn't be gettin' past her to go to the 101 tomorrow, that's for certain."

"The 101? What's that?"

Annie gave her a highly suspicious look. "What's that? You don't know what the 101 is, you're tellin' me?"

Oh, hell. She'd slipped again. "Well, no, I mean—"

"I knew it! You're not well, missus, and I'm sure of it. My own brother, Rory, he got conked on the noggin once, too. Forgot his own name, he did. Even thought we were back in Ireland! Took months for him to get over it. And I don't think you ought to be out in the weather, breathin' in all that dust the cowmen'll be kickin' up."

Dust? Cowmen? Was the 101 a rodeo?

Erin touched the bandage, thinking about Annie's brother, wondering for a moment if the injury really had jarred her brain. Who knew, maybe she really hadn't traveled back seventy years. Maybe this was still 1994 and she'd fallen and cracked her noggin like Rory. Maybe this was all a very creative hallucination her injured brain was conjuring up. Yeah, and maybe, like Dorothy, she'd wake up back in bed in Kansas.

"Annie, I'm okay." Relatively speaking. "I'd just forgotten about the...uh, rodeo, that's all. I've got other things on my mind." Waite MacKinnon, for one, she thought, then impatiently pushed his image from her thoughts.

Of more importance was getting home. Which meant finding J.B.'s key ring to unlock that door. Or finding the other entrances to the tunnels the tour guide had mentioned. They were all over the property, she remembered. A gatehouse, boathouse, guesthouse, artist's studio. She'd seen the other doors from inside the tunnels. They had been locked, too, but it might be easier for her to break in undetected. Sudden inspiration hit, and Erin eyed Annie speculatively. A servant employed by the Munros might have an inkling as to where the tunnel entrances were.

"You're probably right. I should be resting," she said to Annie.

Annie smiled brightly. "Good."

"But, Annie," she said, placing her hand on top of the maid's, "I just won't be able to rest until I get something taken care of. I lost a piece of jewelry last night when I was in the tunnels. Do you think you could help me get it back?"

The maid's smile vanished, and she caught her lower lip with her teeth. She glanced around the room, then said in a whisper, "Mr. Munro...he has a rule. No staff is allowed near the tunnels without his say-so."

"Oh, I'm not asking you to go into the tunnel. I'll do that myself. I just need to know where J.B. keeps his key ring and—"

"Should you be doin' this thing?" she asked, then looked away, her cheeks turning pink. It was clear she felt it presumptuous to comment on her employer's behavior. "It's just that...he'll be angry, and Edith says... Well, I shouldn't be tellin' tales out of the schoolroom, but she says he'll send you away if he catches you down there again."

"Annie, trust me, he's not going to catch me. All I need to know from you is where the other entrances to the tunnels are. Or where J.B. might keep his key ring."

"Other entrances? I...didn't know there were any others."

"What about his key ring?"

The maid shrugged and slowly shook her head.

"What's going on in here?" J.B. stood in the doorway, a scowl etching deep lines into his forehead.

Oh, great. How much of that had he heard? "Nothing. I was just helping Annie put these boxes away."

Erin placed the last one on the shelf, noticing Annie's tensed shoulders and wide eyes. Erin patted her arm reassuringly. "She looked like she could use some help. That's all."

J.B.'s gaze was dubious, but he didn't question her further. "I have to go out for a few hours. Business. I want you to stay away from the stables this afternoon. A ride might tire you," he said, nodding toward the bandage on her head. "I want you at the party tonight, no arguments. And see that your behavior is exemplary. You have a great deal to make up for."

ERIN WAITED UNTIL J.B. was good and gone before she left the room. She found Della's bedroom surprisingly quickly. Locking the door behind her, she went into the connecting bathroom. When she'd stumbled out of the room this morning, there hadn't been time to examine her injury. Now she peeled away the bandage, wincing at her reflection in the mirror. It looked terrible—much worse than it felt, in fact. The bump wasn't large; it was surrounded by an angry purple bruise and bisected by a small, jagged cut. She saw no signs of infection, but wished she could get her hands on a tube of Neosporin, just in case.

And she would, she told herself. As soon as she got home. Then there'd be no more need to worry about J.B. locking her away in an asylum or living in the disguise of an unhappily married Jazz Age floozy, or even playing mistress to a yesteryear hunk.

She could begin her quest right now. The rest of the afternoon was hers: J.B. was out of the house and had unknowingly given her the best idea before leaving. He wanted her to forgo her ride. Wanted her fresh and alert so she could handle damage control. Had he never mentioned the stables, Erin wouldn't have thought of it.

What better way to scout out such an enormous estate? She would save time, and perhaps not arouse as much suspicion, since riding seemed to be part of Della's daily routine. She felt certain she would be out of here soon, but just in case she wasn't, Erin would much rather stay out of J.B.'s bad books. She shuddered, remembering his threat about the asylum.

The trouble was, her only riding experience had been with trail horses she'd rented out by the hour. Still horses were horses.

Flinging off Della's designer dress, Erin stepped out of the torturous heels, then peeled out of the silk hose. She slipped into her jeans, feeling more human the moment she felt the denim slide across her skin.

THE STABLE HAND, wearing a battered cowboy hat, beat-up boots and well-worn Western attire, looked out of place in Munro's pristine stables. He had stepped out from behind a fiery-looking stallion he was grooming, then nudged up the brim of his hat and given her clothing and the panama hat she'd purloined from Della's collection a frown. "Miz Munro? You're here for your ride a bit early, ain't you?"

"Yes, but I just had a whim to ride now."

The man nodded, gave her attire another curious look, then hung the grooming brush on a hook. "Well, I'll get Sophie saddled right up for you. Won't take a minute."

Erin grinned, her nervous stomach settling a bit. Sophie. She could probably handle a Sophie. With a name like that, the horse was probably as easy-going as the two trail horses she had ridden, Butterscotch and Clem.

The cowboy left the stall, latching the gate behind him. Then he loped down the aisle and disappeared into another stall to be greeted by soft whickers of welcome. Erin heard him talking to the horse in a gentle, singsong voice.

There were no soft whickers coming from the horse he'd left, however. In fact, the horse seemed furious at being abandoned midgroom. He pawed the earth with lethal-looking hooves, then glared at Erin and shook his great head, flinging his jet black mane in a spray of anger. Thunderation, Erin read on the shiny brass plaque mounted on the stall door, then shuddered when the horse snorted and gave her another glare. Thank goodness ole Thunder wasn't Della's.

When the stable hand came out of the stall moments later, leading Sophie, a smile quirked at the corners of his mouth. "She's raring to go."

Raring to go and...beautiful. The mare was a gorgeous chestnut color, with a delicate head and a slim body. Her legs were long and her coat was as sleek and shiny as those fancy cars Erin had seen in J.B.'s drive. She was a delight to look at, and aside from a tendency to prance, she seemed as gentle and tame as Thunderation seemed wild.

Erin smiled and forgot for a moment that this horse was simply a means to an end. She stepped up to Sophie and brushed her hand over the horse's neck. "You're a beauty, Sophie, aren't you?" she whispered.

"Oh, she's a beauty, all right. And high-spirited, as always." The man passed Erin the reins, then cupped his hands and bent down to offer her a leg up.

Erin noticed Sophie's saddle wasn't like the ones Butterscotch and Clem had worn. This one was tiny, and there was no horn thingie to grab on to. She glanced at the stable hand, suddenly afraid her ignorance might give her away.

"Something wrong, ma'am?"

"Oh...uh, no. No, nothing's wrong."

Erin heard him mumble something under his breath about little English pie plates. "What did you say?"

He stood straight and scratched his brow. "Aw, I just can't for the life of me understand why you put them silly little Anglish pie plates on these big hosses." Then he shrugged. "But what do I know? It's never given *you* any problems."

Right. Erin wanted to shout for a Western saddle anyway, but he'd bent again and laced his work-roughened hands to help her. Erin shoved her fear aside, reminding herself that begging for a saddle that Della never used might draw even more attention to herself. She put her foot in the man's hand, then reached high and clutched at Sophie's mane with one hand, managing to hold on to the reins with the other. She threw her leg over, then found both stirrups with her feet.

Sophie was just as wonderful to ride as she was to look at. Erin got used to the "Anglish" saddle quickly enough, but nervous as she was about Sophie's size and the distance from the ground, she kept the mare at a gentle canter.

It was finding her way around the estate that proved difficult. The property was huge. In her time there hadn't been all these wide-open spaces on Munro's property. Obviously J.B. had later sectioned off some of the property—maybe even sold some. Equally obvious was the fact that Sophie was used to the wide-open spaces, because that was where she headed immediately. And no amount of dissuasion from Erin was going to change her mind.

Erin decided to let the horse have her head until she was certain they were completely out of the stable hand's earshot. Then, she thought, she'd circle back and find all those outbuildings.

CHAPTER SEVEN

WAITE DISMOUNTED AND dropped Cherokee's reins, watching as the horse dipped its muzzle into the cold creek. He found a large, smooth rock on the bank and sat down, pushing up the brim of his hat and resting his forearms on his bent knees. A solitary flycatcher in a nearby tree screeched and took wing, and Waite followed it with his eyes, squinting at the bright winter sky. The line of trees sheltering the small stream was naked now of the colorful fall foliage it had worn only weeks ago, providing a clear view of the western edge of Waite's new property.

He liked the sight of Oklahoma in winter best of all. Others, mostly the Easterners J.B. had persuaded to populate his town, complained about the stark, colorless landscape. Too flat, too barren, they grumbled. And too damned windy. But to Waite, there was nothing more beautiful than the wide, unbroken plain, stretching out forever beneath winter's pewter sky.

When he'd first laid eyes on the vast prairie he'd been fourteen years old. Waite had made his way west from Virginia, poor as a church mouse but determined to become a wealthy Oklahoma rancher. He'd been full of bravado and completely convinced that everyone who lived in Oklahoma was either a rich oilman or cattle rancher. He would make his fortune by his sixteenth birthday or he'd die trying.

He'd nearly done just that. He looked at Cherokee and remembered another horse—the one he'd decided would be his first test of manhood. All the other hands at the famed 101 Ranch where Waite had hired out had known there was too much devil in the horse to break him to saddle. Not Waite. In his eagerness to prove himself, he'd climbed into the corral with the dangerous animal.

When they'd carried him out again, he was a mass of injuries: a bashed-up face, a broken arm and several broken ribs. When George Miller, the owner of the 101, had approached him afterward, J.B. Munro happened to be at his side. Waite had tried to arrange his battered features into an expression of respect for both men, but had only managed a pained grimace. Miller had shaken his head, and said, "Boy, if you're not the stupidest son of a bitch I've ever known! What the hell were you thinking?"

J.B., however, had grinned down at Waite, an expression that looked like pride in his eyes. "But you rode him for a moment there, didn't you? If you live, son, come see me about a position with Munro Railways. George, old man," he'd added, slapping Miller on the back as they'd walked away, "I value nerve and guts in my organization. I thought you did, too."

Well, he'd lived, of course, but hadn't taken J.B. up on his offer right away. Instead, he'd chosen to stay at the 101 in hopes of soaking up all the knowledge he could. He traveled with the Wild West show and learned a thing or two about trick riding. The other hands had said he was a fool for choosing the harsh life of a cowboy over a position with Munro, but Waite hadn't cared. He'd saved his money, the goal of owning a ranch always close to his heart, he'd spent only what was needed to put himself through college. Then, with a degree in animal husbandry and a minor in business, Waite had come back to Munro, taken the job J.B. had offered and begun saving once again.

Falling in love with Della had changed his mind about a lot of things. He finally understood what the 101 hands and performers had been talking about when they'd complained about their vagabond lives. Della had made him want to settle down, right then—even put all thoughts of a ranch aside—and start a family.

Family. Waite's gaze skipped over to the small creek and he thought of the loved ones he'd lost in the fire at the farm. He remembered it had been a perfect spring day when he'd stood beside their graves and struggled not to cry. The sun had shone gloriously, and the Virginia countryside had been resplendent, washed in its rays, but his heart had been heavy and he'd known he had to move on. Even now, though, on the first day of every spring, he always felt a little sick inside. Maybe that was why he was drawn to this barren winter landscape.

Suddenly the sound and vibration of pounding hooves on the hard, cold ground intruded on Waite's thoughts. Cherokee raised his head, ears twitching, and Waite rose, narrowing his eyes as he waited for the rider to appear over the rise to the west.

A frown drew his brows together when one of J.B.'s Thoroughbreds thundered into view, heading for the creek at a breakneck pace. Its rider was a woman, but she was wearing men's—

"Whoa! Damn it, whoa!" she shouted. "Come on, stop!"

"Oh, for God's sake," Waite muttered when recognition set in. Della. What the hell was the woman doing? She was flopping and bouncing in the saddle as though she'd never ridden a horse in her life. And she knew better than to yell at a horse! Especially a Thoroughbred like Sophie who—

God, the fool woman was going to ride that horse right into a tree! Sprinting for Cherokee, Waite vaulted into the saddle, then watched in amazement as Della somehow managed to turn the horse, and the two went racing off to the east. How she stayed in the saddle was a puzzle to Waite.

Shaking his head, he set out after them. There was no doubt that his stallion could catch the mare, and in moments he and Cherokee were behind them. Della's screams carried back to Waite on the wind, and he was close enough to see the shapely bottom that had inspired so many lustful fantasies in his younger days.

He brought Cherokee alongside them and shouted, "Della, for God's sake, what's—"

Startled, she shrieked and jerked her head around to look at him . . . and let go of the damned reins!

"Damn it! Have you lost your mind?" Waite couldn't quite fathom what he'd just witnessed. The woman who'd taught him the differences between cow ponies and hunters and the art of riding a Thoroughbred, had just dropped the reins of a horse that was streaking across the ground like a whirlwind! His arm shot out to grab her before she lost her seat completely, but he was too late. Her feet came out of the stirrups and she slid backward beyond his reach, then tumbled off the rump of the horse, landing squarely on her backside.

Waite reined in his horse, watching in stunned silence as Sophie galloped off for parts unknown. Quickly he guided Cherokee over to Della, who was lying flat on her back, once again dressed in men's clothing. Yes, her recent behavior was decidedly odd, he mused. He swung down from the saddle and knelt at her side, gently pulling away the hands that covered her face.

She was crying, he noticed with alarm. "Oh God, you're hurt." He quickly pulled off his gloves and took her hands in his. "Della, where are you hurt?"

She didn't answer. She merely shook her head back and forth, squeezed her eyes shut and sobbed even harder.

"Della, talk to me," he urged, forcing back panic. What if the fall had injured her back? "Can you move your legs? Your arms? Here, sit up, bend your knees, move something, goddamn it."

She didn't answer, but she must have heard him through her sobs, because she lifted her heels off the ground, then bent her legs once before dropping them back to the dirt.

"You scared the life out of me," Waite said. He thought of the spectacle he'd just witnessed and shook his head in bewilderment. He'd often seen Della's delight in shocking J.B. and most everyone else in Munro, but he'd never seen anything as foolhardy as this! If he hadn't known it was Della, he'd have sworn another woman had been on that horse.

Alcohol. That was the only explanation.

He leaned in close, trying to get a whiff of her breath.

Della's eyes widened and her sobs abruptly stopped. She shoved at Waite's chest. "Wh-what do you think you're doing?" she demanded warily.

"Checking to see what you've been drinking."

She shoved harder and Waite sat back on his heels. Scrambling up and away from him, she brushed at her backside, then winced. "I...I haven't been drinking anything! It's just—that horse! It wouldn't listen to a word I said."

"Said? How about shouted? You know better than to yell at Sophie."

She sniffed and wiped her cheeks with the sleeve of her shirt, then frowned, looking in the direction her mount had taken. "Is she...deaf or something?"

Waite shook his head at her and stood. "You *have* been drinking, haven't you? Of course she's not deaf. What on earth are you talking about? You know better than to scream at her when she's hellbent for speed.''

"Oh...oh, yeah. Sure, I knew that. I just forgot, that's all.''

So why did he have the feeling that she knew no such thing? Was it because of the spectacle he'd just witnessed—mistakes a horsewoman like Della would never make? Or was it the way she quickly averted her eyes? She was acting the same way she'd behaved this morning inside the fireplace. Jittery. As if she had something to hide. He caught her by the arm and turned her to face him.

"No one who knows horses the way you do forgets how to handle them. Explain that exhibition you just put on, Della. In fact, you've got a lot to explain, don't you? Last night—''

"I just fell off a horse, that's all. Happens to the best of us, doesn't it?''

"No, not to experienced riders like you—'' Just then, blood trickling from the cut on her head caught his eye. "Hell, you're bleeding again.''

Her fingers rose to the wound and came away smeared with crimson. She sighed.

"That's it, isn't it?'' he asked, realization dawning. "Your head. You're in no condition to ride a horse, but you got on Sophie anyway. It's a wonder you were able to stay in the saddle at all.''

"Well . . . yes, you're right," Erin replied. "But you know me. I just wanted to do it, so I did."

"Come with me," Waite said, grabbing her hand and leading her to his horse.

"Are you taking me back to the house?"

"No." He lifted her into the saddle, settling himself behind her, then took her to the copse of trees she'd nearly crashed into. It was a good thing it wasn't far, because her bruised posterior couldn't have taken much more abuse, Erin thought wryly.

Of course her mind was less on her sore rear end than on the fact that she was in Waite Mac-Kinnon's arms. Though she held her back stiff and struggled to keep her thoughts out of the gutter, there was no stopping her little jaunt down sensuality lane. She felt his jaw brush against her hair a couple of times, and imagined, just for the moment, that she really *was* Della. The strong arms that flexed and rubbed against hers as he maneuvered the horse's reins made her wonder about the passionate embraces the two must have shared. And when she wobbled in the saddle and Waite slid an arm beneath her breasts to steady her...well, Della exited the scenario completely. That feeling was there again. The sense of rightness she always felt with him.

Waite stopped the horse near a shallow creek sheltered by overhanging trees, and Erin slid from the saddle, quickly putting some much-needed distance between the two of them. Her legs were shaky, but nevertheless she hurried to the bank, and bent to scoop up water to clean the wound.

"Here." His low voice came from behind her and she glanced around to see him holding out his handkerchief to her.

"Thanks," she said, grabbing it, then hurriedly turning away from the intense expression in his black eyes. Wetting the cloth, she held it firmly against her cut and wondered if the man ever smiled. Granted, she'd only been in his company twice since coming here, but his mood had been strangely intense on both occasions. She found it compelling ... and intimidating.

But it wasn't appropriate to feel compelled. Or intimidated. Nothing, in fact, was appropriate in this situation. She ached to get home. Home to her people, her father. She felt guilty as hell for leaving the house yesterday, no matter how much it had been her family's idea. Now here she was seventy years in the past. Yes, it was time to acknowledge her predicament.

Whatever her feelings toward Waite, Erin wondered if she shouldn't take one last try at persuading him to help her into the tunnels. He hadn't seemed receptive to the idea this morning, but then, she'd backed down because she'd been so preoccupied with the thought of his and Della's affair.

She rinsed out the handkerchief in the cold water, then wrung it out. Steeling herself, she turned to Waite, and was met by the same black, scrutinizing eyes.

"I...need your help, Waite. And if you care anything about me, you'll listen, all right?"

"What is it?"

"I need to find another entrance to the tunnels. Surely one of them will be unlocked." She held up a hand. "No, don't say anything until I'm finished," she begged, "and please stop frowning until you've heard me out!"

Waite frowned but remained silent. Erin gave herself a mental shake. "I still had the locket you gave me. I had it on last night. No, I really did," she added when his look became skeptical.

"I don't want to talk about the damned locket," he said harshly. "If you didn't want it, fine. But the least you could've done was give it back to me, Della."

"I'm...sorry," she murmured, inwardly cursing Della. She could tell that the jewelry had great sentimental value for Waite. Dared she hope that meant he might help her after all? God, how coldhearted that sounded. Her stomach churned with guilt, and she almost decided to give up and not ask another thing of him. But on the heels of her guilt were thoughts of getting home.

"Waite, please, I want it back. It's in that tunnel, and J.B. has locked me out. You could help me get it back, couldn't you? I promise never to ask another thing of you, never to—"

"Stop it." His voice was low and harsh. Then he grabbed her hand and Erin gasped. There was anger in his eyes, and bitterness. His jaw clenched. "You know where the entrances are, damn it. You don't need me. Why the hell do you care about the locket now? It meant nothing to you. You told me so yourself."

"I...I must have lied to you, Waite. Because I promise you, I still had it."

He turned away, dropping her hand. Erin grasped his arm, circling to face him. He stared down at her hand on his arm, one brow lifted. "I don't know what you're up to, Della, but don't drag me into it," he ground out. "No matter what plan you have cooking in that devious little brain of yours, I won't help you. And what the hell does 'I must have lied to you' mean? Don't you know?"

"Waite, please. I don't have a plan. I...I know this is going to sound hard to believe, but...there are lots of things I don't remember about myself. My head. Everything's gone fuzzy since I banged it." She touched the bump and gazed into his eyes, attempting to coat her lie with a look of sincerity.

"You're trying to tell me you have amnesia?" He smirked, shaking off her hand. "Oh, Della, that's too farfetched even for you."

"No, no, Waite. It's not farfetched at all!" *Please!* she wanted to shout, I could tell you a farfetched story that would curl your hair! Not that it needed curl, she noted, taking in the soot black waves that swept back from his forehead and brushed his collar. Soft. It looked soft and healthy. She shook herself again. "It happens all the time. A blow to the head can cause memory gaps."

"And can a blow to the head also cause someone to suddenly gain a heart, a conscience? You knew full well what that locket meant to me, that it was the only thing I had of my mother's, but you coldly rejected the gift. If it meant so little to you then, why do you want it back so badly now?"

"I wish I could explain, but I can't," she replied, flinching at the scorn in his eyes. "I *have* to get it back, Waite. My life depends on it. I can't tell you why, but does that matter? Can't you just help me?"

He studied her with obvious suspicion, his silence inciting a riot of nerves. Erin hated all this duplicity, this subterfuge. Especially with Waite.

And that was another thing she couldn't explain—the sense of connection she felt with him.

It had been his mother's locket. He said he'd given it to Della and she'd rejected it. Erin hated that, too. Oh, this was nuts! She didn't even know Waite—not really. Sure, he made something melt inside her whenever she looked at him, but she shouldn't care so much. She shouldn't care at all.

The only thing that really mattered was that she get the hell out of here, she kept trying to tell herself.

"I won't help you, Della. You're up to something again, and I'm not going to be part of whatever it is. You should know that."

He turned away again and shrugged off her hand. Erin rushed forward and jumped into his path. "But... but I thought we meant something to each other, Waite. You gave me your mother's locket, for heaven's sake. And I just... I mean, I thought..."

"What? What the hell do we mean to each other now? Maybe you're telling the truth, Della. Maybe you do have gaps in your memory. Because if you didn't, you'd remember that you and I are ancient history."

Ancient history? She was confused. "You mean we aren't... I mean... you know..."

"We aren't what?"

She glared at him. "You know...having an affair. Lovers." She was sure her face was crimson, but she refused to back down.

He gave a cynical bark of laughter, then shook his head. "We're not lovers now, and if you want to get right down to it, *love* had nothing to do with what we were back then, either. Weren't those your exact words? The day you and J.B. announced your engagement to the world?"

Erin heard pain in his remarks. He'd been in love with Della, she realized, no matter what he said. And it was obvious Della hadn't returned the sentiment. Erin amended her earlier assessment of the woman. Della had been crazier than she'd realized if she had rejected this man for J.B.

"I know you won't believe this, but I'm really sorry you were hurt," she said, her voice quiet. She hated the thought of wrapping the truth in a fabrication, but it was the only way to convey her feelings without having to offer incredible explanations of who she really was. "Maybe a blow to the head *can* make a heartless person realize how wrong she's been, because I'm truly sorry for what I did to you."

"And I suppose now that you're remorseful and you've seen the light, I should help you get the locket back, is that it? Let me guess why.... You want to sell it to raise money for the orphanage J.B.

funds in Missouri. Or maybe one of his other favorite charities, like that Catholic seminary. No, don't tell me, your head was hit so hard you've decided to join the convent. Ah, yes, I can see it now. Sister Della."

Erin knew it was silly to bristle at Waite's sarcasm. It was Della he was insulting, not her. Still she couldn't help the indignation that rose within her.

"Okay, fine! Don't believe me! But if you're so much better, Mr. Holier-than-Thou, why can't you bend a little? Why can't you help me just this once? You're not exactly the soul of charity yourself, are you? If you were, our 'ancient history' would be just that, wouldn't it?"

Moments of silence passed—silence that Erin struggled to interpret.

Then he smiled, and Erin's heart seemed to forget to beat. She'd never seen him smile, and for one fleeting moment all she could think was, *At least I got to see it before I left.* It deepened the attractive lines at the corners of his eyes, and showed off straight, white teeth. But she wasn't so blinded by the smile that she missed the mockery in it. Damn, but she'd have loved to see him smile at her because he liked what he saw; liked the person she was.

"That bump on the head may have affected your memory, but it certainly didn't make you any less clever. I'm impressed, Della. Whatever your motives for getting back that locket, I have to hand it to you. You're still crafty as hell.

"But not crafty enough. J.B. doesn't want you in those tunnels. And I really would like to be charitable and forgiving, *Sister* Della, but I'm his friend and partner. I won't go against his wishes."

Erin's temper flared. Why was he still J.B's friend? she'd like to know. Damn it, J.B. had married Della when Waite had been in love with her! Waite deserved better friends.

"J.B., J.B., J.B.! You're not his friend and partner! You're...you're his lackey! That's right," she said, when his mouth tightened. "Lackey! If everything happened as you say it did, then the man took away someone you loved, for God's sake! What is it he has over you? Why would you just forget what he did, and bow down to him, do any and everything he wants—"

Waite grabbed her arm so quickly the breath rushed from Erin's lungs. Nose to nose with her, he gritted out, "Get it straight. I am no man's lackey."

"Oh, yeah? If that's true, then you can do this for me," she insisted heatedly. Never one to back down from an argument, she added, "You have to! She— I meant something to you once, Waite. If for no other reason than that and the fact that I've changed—"

"You, Della, will never change. Want proof?" he asked derisively, his black eyes flashing.

Oh, how she wished for proof of her own to wipe that arrogant expression off his too-gorgeous face! But there was none, of course, unless she were to tell him Della's body was in a cave somewhere around here. She gave it a moment's consideration before deciding it would only secure her a one-way ticket on the loony-bin express. Her frustration and anger at the boiling point, she tried to jerk out of his grasp and retorted, "Hell, no. I don't want proof from you! I don't want anything from you! And let go of my arm, you . . . you . . ."

"What, Della?" he demanded, his voice low and seductive as he pulled her closer. "I'm interested to hear what you, of all people, were going to call me."

She couldn't think of a name to call him— couldn't think of anything, in fact, because her breasts were now flush with his rock-solid chest and his arm had snaked around her shoulders to hold her locked against him. The set of his mouth and ferocity in his eyes were at odds with the surprisingly gentle manner in which he caressed her cheek, then stroked her lower lip with his thumb.

Erin froze like an animal blinded by car headlights, her body losing all ability to react. But that wasn't exactly true, was it? Her heart reacted immediately, skipping crazily and pumping blood to her cheeks.

"You're not...going to... I mean, you wouldn't..." she sputtered, hoping...and hoping not.

"Kiss you?"

Her head angled back, she licked her lips, then nodded slowly.

"Yeah, I would." Then his dark head lowered, and before she could shake herself out of the trance, he did just that.

Oh damn, oh damn, oh damn. He was kissing her! She'd wondered and fantasized about this ever since she'd first seen him, and she couldn't for the life of her summon up the will to stop him. It was wrong to string him along just to satisfy her own curiosity, to feel his mouth on hers and his hands caress her. But she did it anyway. She told her conscience to take a hike and simply took what he gave.

And could the man give! Heat pulsed in her blood when he opened his mouth over hers, his tongue stroking her lips, coercing, insisting that she open to him. She allowed him entrance, then closed her eyes when he thrust inside and immediately took up an age-old seductive rhythm.

The kiss wasn't experimental or tentative, as first kisses ought to be. It was raw and sexual and underlaid with a lesson that he meant to teach another woman. For him, it was not a first kiss at all, and Erin was well aware of it.

That fact should have made her wrench away, but her desire was almost painful in its intensity. She pushed closer and wound her arms around his neck, her fingers playing through the silky black strands at his nape even as her tongue joined with his in the dance. Her action seemed to surprise him, and Waite went still for the space of a moment. He broke the kiss and stared down at her, his eyes glazed and his breathing harsh and uneven. He blinked.

"Waite," Erin whispered, feeling bereft. She trailed her fingertips over his firm jaw and rose on her tiptoe to taste the skin there.

She got her wish. He groaned and buried his face in her neck, his mouth tasting her as his hands began to roam.

CHAPTER EIGHT

AN ANGUISHED SOUND tore from Waite's throat, and he trailed kisses up her neck to fuse with her mouth again. His hands traveled from the sweet curve of her waist to her softly rounded shoulders, then stole inside the open collar of her shirt as his tongue continued to claim what had once been his.

His. She was to have been his for a lifetime. And kissing her again after so many years brought back memories of all the plans he'd made for them. A family. He'd wanted to be part of a family again. Della's fingers tunneled through his hair and, as she angled her head to deepen the kiss, as her fine, slender hips writhed against his arousal, he lost his hold on the present and slipped deep into the past, remembering what it was like when they'd been together—when they'd laughed, when they'd kissed, when they'd made love.

It had been like this.

No. Not as good as this. This was better. So damned much better. The woman in his arms seemed so different from the woman she'd been.

Exactly how, he wasn't sure. He only knew that their kisses had been less passionate back then, less urgent. He had loved her but had always settled for what he'd later learned was detached lust. Now, she was acting the way he'd always dreamed she would; as though she was just as swept away as he was.

She slid her fingers inside his shirt, touching, caressing, and he groaned again, rushing to pull open his buttons to afford her better access. Frantically he fumbled for her buttons, wanting, needing, to feel her satin-soft skin against his again, remembering how exquisite it had been when her breasts rubbed against his naked chest ... when he cupped them in his hands, took them into his mouth. God, he remembered.

She'd been his, damn it; his before she'd become J.B.'s wife! That thought jerked him back to reality in a flash of searing guilt, and he tore his mouth from hers. Oh, God, what was he doing? She wasn't his! J.B.'s wife ... She was J.B.'s wife!

He pushed her away.

One hand covering his eyes and his breath rasping in his throat, he shook his head. He'd meant to drive home a lesson...to show her she would never change. How had he allowed it to get so out of hand? And what had possessed him to even think of such an insane act in the first place?

He lowered his hand to look at her. She was trembling, clasping her shirt closed with her fist. Her face was flushed and her lips swollen from the ravishment of his mouth. A tear glistened as it rolled down her cheek.

"Damn it, Della," he said, his voice harsh and raw. He shook his head again, turning away, his hands vicious as they did up the buttons of his shirt. He thought he heard her voice and glanced back over his shoulder. "What!" he snarled.

"N-nothing," she said a bit too quickly, then wiped away the tear with her sleeve. She buttoned up her own shirt, then looked at him.

He imagined it, he was certain, but it struck him that her normally pale green eyes appeared just a shade darker, a shade richer than before. And the expression she regarded him with had a strength and depth that Della wasn't capable of. She cleared her throat, seeming about to say something, then took a step toward him.

"Stay away from me," he ordered. "Just stay the hell away from me, Della."

Her lashes fluttered and she nodded, then turned away. "You don't have to worry about that. I won't come near you again." The words were adamant and filled with conviction. "But do me a favor. Don't call me that anymore. Don't call me Della."

She'd made the same kind of cryptic remark last night. *I'm not Della.* Waite frowned, remembering how changed she'd seemed. And just now, as though she'd been a completely different woman, a woman he'd never met before, Della had come alive at his touch, his kiss. And her eyes . . .

Ridiculous. He might want to believe that the woman who had just turned to flame in his arms wasn't Della Munro, but that didn't alter the fact that she was. That was J.B. Munro's wife standing not three feet away from him, and he was crazy to have forgotten it for even one moment. "You're right. Your name is Mrs. J.B. Munro. Something I accepted a long time ago."

ERIN WAS JUST AS ANGRY as Waite was. And the moment he'd left to find Sophie, she'd chastised herself for allowing that kiss. She perched on a rock next to the creek and pounded her knee with her fist. How could she have been so stupid, so irresponsible, so . . . so self-indulgent that she hadn't given a moment's thought to what kissing Waite would do to him? When had she become such a taker?

The image of his face, stricken and ashamed when he'd pushed her away, came alive in her mind, and Erin squeezed her eyes shut. She was the one who should be ashamed, not him. Because she'd been fully aware of the fact that he'd loved Della. He'd loved her, then lost her to his best friend. Then Erin had rubbed salt in the wound by forgetting who she was supposed to be.

Waite didn't know he'd been kissing someone else. He'd thought it was Della in his arms, Della kissing him back, Della acting as though she'd like to throw him to the ground and have him right there.

Oh, damn, oh damn, oh damn!

Erin wasn't absolving him of all responsibility. He'd started it, she thought a little childishly. He deserved to feel *some* guilt. But Erin had known better, and she should have put a halt to the kiss before it became so...so...

Incredible. She could easily have terminated it, had the kiss been an everyday, garden-variety, vanilla kiss. But it had been like nothing she'd ever experienced before. It had filled her with desire, had made her ache for more than kisses. She'd like to meet the woman who had the willpower to resist him.

And oh, dear Lord, how she'd like to have the chance to test her willpower again.

Erin put her head in her hands. *Home. Dear God, let me go home.*

PLEADING A HEADACHE had gotten Erin nowhere. J.B. had insisted his wife be present at the dinner party he was hosting for several of the civic leaders tonight, no ifs, ands or buts. And he'd demanded that she behave or else. "Him and his sacred image," she muttered under her breath, lifting a forkful of rich pastry to her mouth and wondering which would kill her first—Della's bearded murderer or the fat- and cholesterol-laden foods she'd consumed tonight. Not having eaten since her arrival, Erin had been so hungry that she hadn't cared at first. Now, with the heavy sauces, red meat and too-sweet dessert sitting heavily on her stomach, she found yet another reason to get back home again: her health.

As if on cue, the woman seated next to her lifted an Art Deco clutch purse from her lap and extracted a long cigarette holder. She inserted a cigarette—filterless; what else?—in the holder and lit up, blowing a stream of smoke into Erin's face. "Want one, darling?"

Erin blinked and quelled the urge to fan the toxic cloud. Did Della smoke? Most likely, since everyone else seemed to, but there were limits to how far Erin was willing to take this charade. "No, thank you. Maybe later," she said.

The woman smiled and blew a series of smoke rings. Then, although cocktails had been served before the meal, she reached into her beaded purse again, drawing out a flask this time. Glancing down the length of the table, Erin noted that some of the other women had them, too. Amazing, she thought. She just couldn't get over how much it felt as though she were watching an old movie or had been cast in a period play where everyone but her was in character.

Easy for them, Erin thought. They didn't have to play the part of Della Munro. She had to take on the personality of a floozy, pretend to be the wife of a man who wanted her put away, a woman of loose morals whose ex-lover sneered at her and a woman believed dead by a bearded man who'd tried to murder her. Which was the more challenging role?

She hadn't thought about the murderer until this evening because she'd been too busy trying to find a way into the tunnels. But now that Erin wasn't so sure she could get back to the nineties anytime soon, the prospect of Della's killer coming after her became all too real. What if the man was one of J.B.'s business associates? What if he'd been one of the guests tonight? Wouldn't he have been one shocked puppy to see Della walking around, and with no bruises on her neck to show for all his hard work?

Thank God that hadn't been the case—there were no beards in sight this evening. But how long would Erin's luck hold out?

She glanced down the length of the table and her eyes locked with J.B.'s. Raising her hand to her forehead and mimicking a pained look, she mouthed, "Headache, J.B. Please?" He shook his head and sent her a look that said, "In your dreams."

Erin dropped her hand to her lap and sighed, her gaze wandering around the table and finding Waite.

Waite. The man had been devastating in riding clothes, but dressed in evening finery, he was mouthwatering. His broad shoulders emphasized the fit of the elegantly cut striped suitcoat, the snowy wing shirt collar contrasted with his deeply tanned skin and black hair, and the handsome silk tie and matching handkerchief that peeked from his front pocket were designed to attract female attention. They most certainly attracted Erin's. And a few of the other women's, she noted, suffering an inappropriate pang of jealousy. The woman next to him could hardly keep her bejeweled hands off him, and the one seated directly across from him looked as though she wanted to hike her skirt, climb over the table and sit in his lap.

When Waite reached for the crystal water goblet in front of him, and caught Erin staring, she all but jumped. Heat flooded her face and she glanced away quickly, but not before noticing the scowl he gave her. *Just stay the hell away from me,* she remembered him saying.

Sounds like a plan, she wanted to retaliate. She'd been foolhardy to step too close to the fire this afternoon, but Erin was a quick study. And she'd picked up immediately on the fact that Waite MacKinnon was a raging sexual inferno.

The sound of voices in the foyer just outside the formal dining room caught Erin's attention, and she glanced back over her shoulder to see one of the servants talking to a woman. Plainly dressed in comparison to the peacocks seated at the table, she was tearfully asking to speak to J.B. When the butler tried to explain that wasn't possible, the woman's voice grew louder, more insistent. She noticed Erin watching her then, and suddenly stopped in midsentence. She lifted her chin and shot Erin a venomous look.

Oh, no! Erin thought. *What now?*

The more the butler tried to put the woman off, the more determined she became. He finally gave up, left the woman in the foyer, and strode back into the dining room and to J.B.'s side. J.B. frowned as the man whispered to him, then rose from his seat, making excuses to his guests. He followed the butler into the foyer.

Something was up, Erin realized. Something big. It was clear J.B. had been intent on getting rid of the woman, but after only a few loudly whispered remarks from the woman, he glared over his shoulder at Erin. Erin caught snatches of the conversation and didn't like the sound of it.

My husband… Your wife…

No, she didn't like the sound of it one bit. Swiveling around in her seat, she was met by silence and the quizzical expressions on the faces of the guests. Harrison Wyndham, the Boston banker, seemed most interested of all. Erin prayed that J.B.'s desire for damage control would keep him from exploding. Surely he would squelch this, if for no other reason than his important business deal.

But it appeared that she was to have no luck on that front. J.B.'s footsteps sounded like a death knell as he strode across the marble foyer and back into the dining room.

"Della," he said, making little attempt to mask his anger. "We have a visitor we need to speak with. You'll excuse us," he added for the benefit of his guests. Then he grasped her arm and pulled her up. What she would have given to be able to take the woman up on that offer of a cigarette, now that she was about to face a firing squad, but J.B. didn't give her the time to ask. He had her out of her chair and striding toward his office before she or any of the dinner guests had known what hit them. Once inside, with the door closed behind them, J.B. whipped out his linen handkerchief for the woman, who had fallen tearfully into a chair, and Erin no longer had to fake a headache.

"Explain yourself, wife," J.B. demanded through gritted teeth. He walked toward his massive oak desk and sat facing her as he pulled a set of keys from his pocket and unlocked a drawer. He extracted a leather-bound book and flung it open. "Explain yourself to me and this poor woman."

Erin shook her head slowly. "I...don't know this woman," she stated quietly.

The woman raised her pretty, tear-streaked face from the linen cloth. Her hands trembled and her eyes were full of equal parts animosity and heartbreak. Her cloche hat was mouse brown and didn't match her well-worn black coat. On her feet were scuffed, down-at-the-heel shoes, and peeking out below the hem of her coat was a faded yellow dress, too thin for winter wear.

An inexplicable surge of guilt washed through Erin. She was outfitted to the nines in Della's silk Lanvin evening dress. The long string of pearls she'd chosen to wear with it suddenly seemed distasteful and gaudy, the elegant T-strap heels frivolous. But they were Della's, she reminded herself, not hers. Just as it was Della's crime she was about to be accused of.

"But you know my husband, Roy, don't you?" The woman pulled a photograph from her coat pocket and held it out to Erin. "You know him very well. He told me so... He said—" her voice broke, becoming a tortured whisper "—he loved you. C-couldn't...live with the thought that y-you... didn't love him, too. So he left town. Left me and the children...." She sniffed and dabbed at her eyes with the handkerchief, then gazed up at Erin. "I...just have to know if he was...telling the truth."

Damn you, Della, Erin thought, her heart rending in two for the woman. *If you weren't dead already I'd strangle you myself!*

But wait a minute. Della *was* dead. And maybe this Roy was her killer. Unrequited love was as good a motive as any. Hadn't the woman said that her husband had left town? Maybe it wasn't because he couldn't live with the fact that Della had spurned his affections. Maybe he feared prison, or even a death sentence. Erin reached for the photo, wondering if she'd found a piece of the puzzle.

But the man had no beard and no other resemblance to the murderer. He was blond instead of dark, lean instead of large-framed. Erin suffered a moment's disappointment, but it fled the second her gaze lighted on the anguished wife again. The poor woman had it bad enough being married to an adulterous jerk, but if he'd been a murderer as well, it would have been even worse.

"Do you know the man, Della?"

Erin hadn't realized how quiet the room had become until J.B.'s angry voice cracked the silence. His eyes were filled with that same anger, but there was something else, as well. The same thing, in fact, that had been in the woman's expression. Hope. Just as the woman had come here in the hope that her husband hadn't betrayed their vows, J.B. hoped it wasn't true. He might not consciously realize it, but it was visible in his eyes.

He pulled a pen from the desk drawer and nodded toward the open book in front of him. "I want to help this woman, but first I need to know if what she says is true. I need to hear it from you."

"Oh, no! I don't want no money from you, Mr. Munro," the woman objected loudly, jumping up from her chair. She tilted her chin at a prideful angle. "I didn't come here for that." She turned to Erin, her eyes beseeching. "I just had to know if Roy was telling the truth."

Erin swallowed hard, glancing from the wife to J.B., then back again. *The truth? It was* the truth, wasn't it? It had to be! Della would have done this. Of course, she would have. The situation had her signature all over it. Erin was sick to death of all the lies, but this wouldn't actually be lying, would it?

Though she couldn't be absolutely certain Della had done it, there was a better-than-even chance she had. Hell, even J.B. believed it, and had immediately pulled out the old checkbook.

And besides, this woman needed the money in the worst way, no matter who Roy, the jerk, had fooled around with. She had children to feed and clothe. Her family shouldn't have to suffer for what her husband had done. Erin had the power to make sure they wouldn't, and even if the man had lied about having had an affair with Della, Erin simply couldn't stand by and not do something!

"Della . . ."

She turned back to J.B., ready to confess in Della's place—until she met that look in his eyes again. Oh, Lord, no matter what she did, someone was going to pay, and pay dearly. Again she wished Della hadn't already met her Maker. She should be the one paying, not these two. And she should also be the one facing the music, Erin thought, noting J.B.'s tic was acting up again.

It reminded her of J.B.'s threat, and her stomach twisted in knots. One more stunt and she was going to find herself put away in an asylum. Her head pounded harder, and Erin chewed her lower lip. Oh, how she wanted to smash through the locked door and run—anywhere, just as long as it was miles away from here. What she would give to be back home, faced with decisions she could handle.

"Your answer, Della," J.B. commanded.

"Please, I ... don't know what to say to you, either of you...."

J.B. made a disgusted sound and rubbed at the tic in his cheek. "The truth. That shouldn't be so difficult."

"But I don't know the truth!" she blurted out.

The woman's forehead creased in surprise. J.B. glowered. "Della..."

"Pay her the money, J.B. She needs it and you know it. I'll admit to it if you—"

"No!" the woman said. She strode to J.B.'s desk. "Please put the draft away, Mr. Munro. I wouldn't think—"

Erin moved, too, seeming to take the woman by surprise again when she grabbed her arm. "Take it. You have to. What about your kids? Listen, pride won't pay your bills, feed your family! You need—"

"I don't need your charity, Mrs. Munro!" She shrugged off Erin's hand and backed away, her eyes welling with tears again. "I won't take anything from you!"

"Come on, forget about what he did and just—"

"No, I want only—"

"And take the money—"

"—to know if my Roy—"

"For your kids if nothing else—"

"Here, now! Stop it! Both of you!" J.B. shouted, pounding his fist on the burled-walnut desk. It caught their attention, and the women's heads turned. He sighed loudly and raked a hand through his hair. "This seems to be getting us nowhere."

"J.B., I said yes, okay? I did it, so just write—"

"No!" the woman insisted.

"Be quiet," J.B. ordered. "Mrs. Tompkins, I need to speak alone with my wife." He came out from behind the desk, passed them and unlocked the office door. "If you wouldn't mind, could you please step outside for a moment?"

She did as requested, shooting Erin a baffled look on her way out. J.B. closed the door and approached Erin, indicating that she should sit in the chair behind her. He took the one facing her.

"You weren't with this man, were you?" he asked quietly, taking her hand in his.

Erin remembered holding J.B.'s hand when he'd been dying. She remembered how he'd called out Della's name and asked for her forgiveness, and she thought of how he would soon learn that his wife was dead. No matter what she'd been in this life, she'd been his wife—maybe even someone he'd loved. That meant something. Erin wasn't quite sure what, but she knew there was a connection between the two that brought a look of sadness and pain to his eyes. Della might have been guilty of this thing, but Erin had the power to alleviate some of J.B.'s pain. It would mean meddling, taking matters into her own hands. She found she simply couldn't not do it.

"No," she whispered, and felt somewhere deep in her heart that it was the truth. "No, I wasn't."

He nodded, as though he believed her.

"But he was with *someone,* J.B. And he left that woman and her children. You'll help her, won't you?"

"Yes," he answered with a promptness that made Erin wonder if he'd planned to do that all along. He squeezed her hand lightly, surprising Erin. She tried to interpret the gesture. Was it husbandly? Fatherly? Whatever it was, it was gentle and tender, and Erin wondered suddenly if J.B. and Della's relationship could be healthier than she'd thought. He'd made a comment this morning, something about not being a true husband, and Erin had just assumed that meant they weren't intimate with each other. But separate bedrooms didn't necessarily mean they didn't sleep together, and she was filled with apprehension.

"I want this sudden concern for someone other than yourself to be genuine, Della. But you must understand that it takes me by surprise."

"Yes, I do." She cleared her throat, not knowing if she would regret what she'd just done. The woman and her children deserved help, but, odd as it sounded, Erin didn't necessarily want to heal the rift in Della and J.B.'s relationship. It could mean a whole new set of problems for her.

"I wouldn't count on a personality turnaround, if I were you," Erin said, aiming for sarcasm, but not sure she had struck the right note. "Just call it an aberration," she added.

J.B. sighed and let go of her hand, then rose, turning away from her. He walked toward the door and unlocked it. As he opened it, he said, "You're right... an aberration. And I promised I'd never speak about what happened again. I'll keep that vow to you. It's the least I can do for the kindness you've shown tonight."

CHAPTER NINE

ERIN AWOKE TO THE SOUND of a radio playing softly. This time she recognized immediately where she was, and what the date was. It would have been impossible to mistake the man crooning "A Rainbow on My Shoulder" for Neil Diamond or Michael Bolton. She sighed, sat up in bed and pushed her hair out of her face.

Day two, she thought, and shook her head.

After the scene in J.B.'s office last night, Erin and he had reached a truce of sorts. He hadn't let down his guard so much that she could escape to her room, but at least the remainder of the dinner party wasn't as fraught with tension as the beginning. He kept a watchful eye on Erin, but frowned at her less. Toward the end of the night she even caught him smiling and joking with his guests. The rest of the party followed his lead, and all the stares and raised brows directed at her when she and J.B. returned from his office eventually disappeared. Erin supposed the guests didn't have to know the details to figure out what had happened in that office.

She squinted at the clock across the room, then jumped out of bed. Eleven o'clock! The party had continued into the wee hours, so she supposed she could be forgiven, but Erin had never slept so late in her life! She hurried into Della's opulent bathroom, remembering how the tour guide had gone on and on about the luxuries in this household compared to those of common folk in this era. For all that the urban areas of the country enjoyed modern conveniences like indoor plumbing and radios and cars, this was Oklahoma. People who weren't of J. B. Munro's class—the farmers and oil field and railroad workers—wouldn't know a Pierce-Arrow automobile if it ran over them, and they certainly didn't own anything as expensive or frivolous as a radio.

As she showered, Erin worried about the abandoned wife again. J.B. had assured her that he would find a way to take care of the woman's financial needs, but he'd refused to let Erin "lie" by admitting she was involved with her husband. But what if Erin's truth wasn't Della's? What if it really had happened and the woman found proof, then brought it to J.B.? Was there a padded room in Erin's future? More misery for J.B. and for Roy's wife?

Well, she would just have to deal with it when the time came. Besides, if her plan to get the locket worked out soon, there would be no need to worry at all.

Erin was going to try to find her way into the tunnels again tonight after everyone was asleep. Her strategy involved sneaking out of the mansion and searching all the buildings the guide had mentioned as having access to the tunnels. And this time she knew where those structures were. She'd noticed them when Waite had brought her back to the main house yesterday.

Waite. She'd learned last night that he was coming along with her, J.B. and Wyndham to the 101 Ranch today.

She'd done her damnedest to keep her eyes off him after returning to the dinner party last night, but her strength of will had failed her. She'd just had to know; just had to see if there would be disapproval in his eyes, reproach for what he guessed Della had done. It was another woman's shame, but that hadn't kept Erin from taking responsibility for it, any more than she could slough off accountability with Waite.

Meeting his gaze, she'd lifted her chin and sent a mental challenge, but there had been no censure in his expression. None for her, at least. He'd stared back at her with a clenched jaw, and the only emotion she could see in the depths of his beautiful dark eyes had been self-recrimination.

Owning up to Della's guilt had been difficult enough for Erin but having kissed Waite, the guilt now belonged to her. And that was worse. The shame tasted like ashes in her mouth, and Erin spent the rest of the night avoiding his eyes. She hadn't been able to escape thoughts of him, though. Thoughts too carnal in nature for her peace of mind.

Eventually, the party guests had trailed out of the dining room and into a large parlor. Erin had joined the cluster of women, and struggled to focus her attention on their chatter. It wasn't as though their conversation was boring. On the contrary, it had been rather intriguing to listen to the women discussing a strange new form of surgery called "face-lifting," shopping trips to New York and naughty stage plays they'd attended and had been delightfully shocked by.

Then, when the women's dialogue had taken a decidedly sexual turn toward Dr. Freud and his theory that sex was the central and pervasive force that moved mankind, Erin became a helpless hostage to libidinous thoughts about a man she'd vowed to put out of her mind. One of the women spoke of seeing an analyst in Europe who had suggested that if she were to be well and happy, she must obey her libido. Another adamantly agreed, saying an uninhibited sex life was the first requirement for mental health, according to her New York analyst.

While shooting Erin looks insinuating that *she* must know all about uninhibited sex, they had batted back and forth their various sexual theories until Erin had wanted to run screaming from the parlor—but only after grabbing Waite by the arm and taking him along with her. She couldn't stop thinking about their one kiss, couldn't get over how willing she'd been to forget who she was, where she was from and the fact that she had to get back. Most of all, she couldn't put an end to her traitorous urges. Though Erin hadn't ventured a single glance in Waite's direction for the remainder of the party, she'd felt his gaze on *her*. And God help her, even knowing the danger in it, she'd wanted to feel more than that.

This morning she had awakened with the thought that if Freud was right, she was going to be a mental wreck in no time. She'd had dreams of Waite last night, dreams during which she had acted on her urges. She had thrown control to the wind and had made love with him, not thinking for a moment about J.B. or Della or returning home to her father. She had reveled in the freedom to touch and caress him, to feel him love her. She shook her head. It was just a dream, she reminded herself, toweling off from her shower, then dressing in another of Della's outfits for the trip to the 101. A dream that hadn't a prayer of ever coming true.

SHE WAS DOING IT AGAIN, damn it! Acting as though she'd never seen the inside of J.B.'s Packard when she'd been the one to help pick it out. Waite watched Della through narrowed eyes from his corner of the back seat. She glanced down at the floorboard, then, with the toe of one shoe, lifted the small rug that covered it and peered at it, inspecting it like someone about to purchase the automobile.

She'd been staring at the car from the moment J.B. had seated her across from Waite and closed the door, then joined Wyndham in the front. Brushing her fingers over the leather upholstery, she'd surreptitiously peeked over the seat when J.B. hit the starter button. Her eyes had widened almost imperceptibly, and a small childlike smile of delight had played about her lips. But when she ventured a look at him out of the corner of her eye, the delight had vanished. He'd met her glance with a lifted brow, and she'd folded her hands in her lap and sat staring straight ahead, still as a statue for the rest of the trip.

It shouldn't have irritated him, but it did. He couldn't explain why, exactly, but Della paying attention to the rules, Della doing as bidden, made him uneasy. It just wasn't... Well, hell, it wasn't Della. He likened it to her behavior when she and J.B. had reappeared at the dinner party last night. Waite had expected to see the usual expression of rebellion and outright defiance on her face, or maybe a mocking, self-satisfied smile. Though she'd almost dared him to cut her down with a censorious look, he'd seen remorse in her expression, and it had reminded him of his own.

Waite glanced out at the barren plain as they neared the 101, suddenly realizing why he was irritated. He wanted everything to remain as it had always been before she'd come up out of the tunnels the other night. He didn't want Della to gain a heart and a conscience, just as he hadn't wanted to experience the tumult he'd felt when he'd held her in his arms. The old Della was easy to dismiss from his thoughts—but not the woman she seemed to have become.

Now she was what, as a young man, blinded by love and lust, he had perceived her to be. He'd been wrong, of course, but that had been what he'd wanted to see.

He didn't like it. Seeing glimmers of the woman he'd desired her to be made him angry, in fact. He'd lost that woman...actually had truly never had her. It rankled to know that a bump on the head might be responsible for changing Della into his old ideal. It rankled to feel the attraction again. It had been dead for so many years, destroyed when she'd so callously spurned the love he'd offered. It was insane that he found himself drawn to Della again, but he could hardly deny it. Since he'd kissed her yesterday, he'd found it impossible to tear her out of his thoughts.

They turned into the 101 just in time to interrupt those dangerous thoughts. Even thinking about Della as anything other than his friend's wife was alarming.

J.B. cut the Packard's engine and glanced over his shoulder at Waite with a grin. He nodded toward the beautiful, three-story white ranch house, "Bring back memories?"

"A bunch," Waite replied, his lips curving upward as he caught sight of his former boss, George Miller. What a picture the rancher made, dressed in cowboy regalia and leaning indolently against one of the Grecian columns.

J.B. turned to the man seated in the front with him, clapping him jovially on the arm. "You won't be sorry you decided to come along for this, Harrison. Those cronies of yours in Boston will be jealous as hell that you got to see a real Wild West show.''

"These shows travel, you know. Saw one like it only last spring," the banker commented with a bored look.

Waite held in a chuckle. The man didn't fool him for a second. J.B. neither, judging from the discreet wink he sent Waite.

"Ah, been to one, have you? Well, we'll just have to see how it compares to the real thing, won't we?"

Wyndham harrumphed and opened his door. J.B. chuckled and got out of the Packard, then helped Della out. Waite followed suit, noting that she was once again taking in her surroundings as though they were new to her. What was going on? Could her amnesia story be genuine? She was more wide-eyed than old Wyndham, ogling some of the performers standing nearby. Her gaze settled on the Indians and their colorful headdresses, and she seemed not to recognize the cowgirls she'd met on past visits. Her head swiveled this way and that, as if she were trying to get her bearings, as she walked alongside J.B. up to the porch of the "White House," as Miller's home had been dubbed.

"Munro, you old dog, you! What'd it take to get your sorry hide out of that mansion for a visit with us saddle tramps—news that Will and Tom are here?'' Miller said with an exaggerated drawl as he shook J.B.'s hand.

Wyndham, who stood next to Waite, cocked a brow at Waite and asked quietly, "Will and Tom?"

"Rogers and Mix," he answered, then hid a wry grin when the banker's mouth gaped. "Mr. Miller," Waite said, stepping forward with his hand outstretched. "Good to see you again, sir."

"*Mister* Miller," George hooted, shaking his hand. "*Sir.* This from the man who could buy and sell me any day of the week and twice on Sunday. Can I talk you into doing a little bronc-busting for us today, MacKinnon?" he asked with a wide grin. He pointed at Waite and in a stage whisper to Wyndham, said, "This one used to work for me, you know."

Wyndham seemed impressed, which was just as J.B. and Miller had planned it. Miller was a show-man through and through, and had jumped at the opportunity to help J.B. and Waite out in this business matter. For all that he liked to act as if he were a simple rancher, the house behind him told a different story. George had built an empire out of bringing the romance of the West to the rest of the world. And he was just as concerned about the economy in Oklahoma as J.B. was.

Miller took Della's hand and lifted it to his lips. "Mrs. Munro. Dad blame it if I'm not gonna have to put blinders on my cowboys again! You look as lovely as ever.''

Her smile was shy and pretty, and Waite became uneasy again. There wasn't a shy bone in that woman's body, damn it. No matter how much J.B. might have demanded that she do some acting today, too, Della wouldn't have agreed to it. In fact, the very suggestion would have pushed her to do the opposite.

She caught him staring, scowling at her, and the smile abruptly vanished. It was only after she'd turned away that he realized his hands were balled into fists at his sides. Ridiculous. Crazy that he should care whether she smiled or not, whether the smile was comely or conniving, bashful or bold as brass. Della Munro was none of his concern. And it was dangerous to think otherwise.

Miller introduced a visibly intrigued Wyndham to some of the performers, then they were all off to the arena where the show would soon begin. Most of Munro City had shown up to watch the spectacle, as well, and once everyone was seated in the stands and the performance got off to a roaring start with a parade of cowboys and cowgirls, Indians, a troop of Cossacks and even a trio of burlesquing harlequins, Waite tried to relax and enjoy it.

But he couldn't shake the uncomfortable feeling that nagged at the edges of his mind. The cowboy shoot-outs and Indian war dances, the trick riders and bareback shooters weren't enough to distract him from thoughts of the woman he'd ridden next to today. And it wasn't just her actions that disturbed him. There was something else.

Her eyes *were* a darker green now. Damn it, they were! He hadn't imagined it yesterday, it was the truth. He ought to know. It seemed as if he'd spent more time looking at her in the past two days than he had the entire time they'd been lovers.

ASIDE FROM THE SCOWLS and frowns and curious looks she'd received from Waite all day, Erin was having the time of her life. Whatever his problem was, she had decided to ignore it. This was too much fun for his black mood to bother her.

When Annie had mentioned the trip to the 101 Ranch, Erin had pictured looking at horses and cows in a corral, maybe watching a cowboy break a horse or lasso a steer or two. A rodeo of some sort. Erin had never been to one, but knew from movies and TV what they were like.

But this was like no rodeo or mere visit to a ranch Erin could ever have imagined. Along with the rest of the crowd, she'd been astounded by the skillful trick riders and sharpshooters, awestricken by the pageantry of the Cossacks and Oriental dance groups, and enthralled with the mini stage-shows depicting pioneer life on the plains of Oklahoma. Added to that there had been circus acts, with clowns and elephants, camels and buffalo.

She particularly loved the women riders. Dressed up Annie Oakley-style, one of them stood in the saddle firing a rifle at a target while her horse, a gorgeous palomino, thundered across the arena. She appeared to fall, and Erin gasped and stood, almost jumping out of the stands to help her before she saw that the woman had planned it that way. The rider hadn't hit the ground at all; she was hanging on with one boot in the stirrup, still firing away at the target, her backside mere inches from the ground!

Erin was enjoying today as she'd enjoyed few others. And she wasn't about to allow either J.B. *or* Waite to put a damper on her fun. She wished her aunt and parents could see her now. This was history she was witnessing, history that she was smack-dab in the middle of! That fact added even more excitement. Besides, after two hellish days of pretending to be the infamous Della, she was grateful for the chance to just cut loose.

Her excitement fled and tension made her nerves crackle when the next event got under way. All she could think of as she watched cowboys jump off their horses, then try to wrestle steers with deadly sharp horns to the ground, was what horrible wounds the animals could inflict. And just how much help would 1920s medicine be to the poor victim? Bulldogging, they called this event, but it might just as well have been called suicide. She and the crowd held their breath, thrilled by the cowboys' strength and agility, but on the edge of their seats with terror, should anything go—

It happened. And damn it, she knew it would! The audience shrieked when the last cowboy leapt from his horse, grabbed the steer, but then was shaken off and flung to the ground by the beast. Erin shot to her feet. In horror, she watched as the steer, refusing to be distracted by a rodeo clown, went after the fallen cowboy again, slamming him in the chest so hard that Erin could have sworn she felt the impact herself. Finally the steer was driven away by several of the other performers, but as the cowboy was taken out of the arena, Erin couldn't tell if he'd simply had the wind knocked out of him or something worse. But she didn't waste a moment more thinking it over.

Twenties medicine was all she could think about as she scrambled past stunned spectators to get to the end of the row where she, J.B., Waite and the banker were seated. If he hadn't just had the breath knocked out of him, if his heart had stopped—as

Erin suspected, judging by the force of the impact—no one in the 1920s would know how to save him.

"Della!" J.B. shouted, and jerking around, she saw concern on his face. "Are you ill?"

"Yes," she lied. Yes, that could happen. She cradled her stomach with her arms and grimaced. "I...just can't watch this." Then she took the bleachers two at a time, leapt to the ground and rushed behind them, quickly scanning the area in hopes of spotting a medical tent of some sort.

Within moments, she'd found it. Two men were carrying the cowboy into the tent, several of the other performers crowding in after them. As she made a dash for it she could hear that the show had gone on—the band had struck up a new tune and horses' hooves pounded the ground. Almost tripping in Della's ridiculous heels, she yanked them off and continued running. When she reached the tent, she shoved her way past the small throng of cowboys, dancers, Indians, even George Miller himself, until she saw a man leaning over the table where the cowboy lay. With an odd-looking ancestor of the stethoscope in his ears, he was listening to the cowboy's heart. He glanced up at Miller and shook his head. "His heart's stopped, George. Nothing more I can—"

"No! Get away!" Erin shouted, and rushed forward. She threw down her shoes and pushed the doctor aside. Grabbing the cowboy's arm, she checked for a pulse and, as she'd expected, found none. Quick as lightning she did a cursory check for broken ribs, then started CPR.

"Here now!" the doctor exclaimed when she began pumping his chest with the heels of her hands. "What do you think you're up to, young lady?"

"Just give me some room." She pulled the cowboy's jaw forward instead of tilting his head back— worried that he might have suffered damage to the spine. Then she pinched his nose closed and blew into his mouth. All around her were exclamations from the onlookers, the doctor's the loudest of all. "Wha— Here now, I said!" He grabbed her arm when she started to pump his chest again.

"Back off," Erin growled, shooting the man a ferocious look. "Just back the hell off!"

His mouth went slack and he did as she ordered. A hush descended over the tent full of people, and Erin turned back to the boy, pumping his chest, then filling his lungs with air and checking for a pulse every few minutes.

Again. Again. *Come on, come on.... Breathe, guy, breathe.* There was only so much time before brain damage would occur. Again. Again. *Please, God.*

Erin knew the moment she felt him inhale, knew the moment his breath met hers, that God had been listening, and her throat went tight with emotion. She reared back and watched the miracle—one she'd witnessed so many times before: the bluish-tinged skin transforming to a healthy pink. She stroked his cheek with her fingertips, her heart banging crazily as she waited for his eyes to open.

The doctor rushed to the other side of the table, gave Erin a dazed look. "Clint?" he said. "Clinton, boy?"

Clint coughed and gave a quiet groan, then his eyes fluttered open.

"*Yes!*" she cried, and heard gasps from the crowd behind her.

One of the cowboys said, "I'll be goddamned," then whooped and slapped his knee.

Erin could only smile as she stroked the boy's cheek. "You with me?" she asked, the fingers of her free hand instinctively reaching to check his pulse again. The question was unnecessary, of course, and so was feeling for the pulse again. But he'd come so close to dying, Erin needed reassurance from every sign of life she could find.

His expression, both puzzled and pained, the boy croaked out, "Yes . . . yes, ma'am."

"God almighty," the doctor breathed, his stunned gaze flipping back and forth between Erin and Clint. He put his hand on the boy's chest, then shook his head. "What was that you did?"

George Miller appeared at her side. "Mrs. Munro...?" he whispered in an awed voice, removing his cowboy hat and looking down at Clint, who was now trying to sit up. Good, Erin thought. No trauma to the spine, it seemed.

Then she looked up at Miller. She'd been running on adrenaline, frantic to perform a medical procedure she knew wasn't recognized at this time. But how to explain it? She'd acted on instinct, not even pausing to think about the repercussions.

She backed away from the table, her gaze swinging from Miller to the doctor, then the knot of performers crowded behind her. She reached for her discarded shoes. "It was...uh...just something I heard about...uh...in Europe," she muttered.

The doctor and rancher exchanged incredulous looks.

"Really... I heard about it there." She picked up the shoes, then thought about J.B. If this got back to him... Well...she could do without more complications. "Can I...talk to you outside, Mr. Miller?"

The man nodded slowly, disbelief still etched on his face, and followed her out.

"I don't know what to say, Mrs. Munro." He still held his hat in his hands, still looked as though he'd been poleaxed. "That thing you did back there... I've never seen the likes of it."

"I know. But, really... I overheard a doctor in Europe talking about it... a-at a party J.B. and I once attended. I'd forgotten about it, actually. And I just, well, when I saw Clint hit by the steer... I thought maybe it would work. That's all."

He shook his head. "That was a miracle you performed. Clint was a dead man and you—"

"No. No, it was just something I remembered. And, Mr. Miller, I want you to promise me something."

"Well, yes, ma'am. I owe you a debt of gratitude, of course."

"Could we just keep this our little secret?"

He frowned. "Why?"

"I have my reasons. Personal reasons. Like you said, you owe me. And this will be payment of that debt. Just... don't mention it to J.B."

"Well... all right, but—"

"Thank you, Mr. Miller." Erin breathed a sigh of relief and gave his hand a grateful squeeze. "I know it's strange, but...well, thank you." Then she put on her shoes and took off like a shot for the stands.

WAITE STEPPED OUT OF the tent and went over to George Miller's side. His ex-boss was scratching his head, his baffled gaze riveted to Della's retreating form. When she was out of sight, George turned to look at him. "My stars and little catfish," he said with a half chuckle. "I've seen some sights in my life, but never anything like that. Did you see all of it?"

"Saw enough."

"What do you make of it?"

What did Waite make of it? He made that Della was lying for one thing.

Again.

He'd overheard her conversation with George, and he knew that Della had never attended a party with J.B. in Europe. She'd never even been there at all. Before becoming J.B.'s wife, Della had been content with traveling in this country. Since they'd been married, she'd planned one European trip after another, only to have them canceled by J.B. for "misbehavior."

"I don't know, George. It was like nothing I've ever seen."

George shook his head, then put his hat back on. For all his puzzlement, his eyes were also bright with relief over his bulldogger's rescue. "Saved his life," he said in quiet bemusement. Then he left Waite and made his way back inside the tent.

The boy had been dead, and Della had brought him back. She'd breathed into his mouth, pushed at his chest, his heart. It was a powerful image; one Waite would never forget. To think it was possible to bring someone back from the gates of heaven— or the threshold of hell—by simply sharing one's breath...

Hell, he had seen it with his own two eyes and he still didn't believe it! Especially of Della Munro. That was compassion he'd witnessed today. Compassion and mercy and...caring. He couldn't shake the picture of her placing her hand, a hand that trembled, on the boy's cheek.

CHAPTER TEN

"WHEN CAN WE GO HOME, J.B.?" Erin asked when she was seated in the stands again.

"Go home?" He frowned. "Are you going to tell me seeing that accident gave you the vapors?"

"I'm all right. But it *has* been a long day and I'd just like to leave."

His frown deepened and he cut her off with, "You've never been a weak sister, Della, so don't become one now. This is business. Just look at Wyndham," he whispered. "His eyes have been bulging out of his head since we got here. I want him to feel the full effect, and that won't happen until the last act. Will Rogers and Tom Mix are about to make their appearance, and I want—"

"Wait a minute. Where's Waite?" Erin interrupted. He'd been seated between J.B. and Wyndham. Now his seat was ominously empty. She quickly glanced about the stands, hoping he'd just changed seats and hadn't followed her—hadn't seen what she'd done....

"Since he left right after you did, I suppose he went to ask after the cowboy's condition. He still considers these people family, you know, after working here so long. Probably knows the boy well."

That was right. Waite had worked here. George Miller had mentioned it when they'd first arrived. So Waite probably *had* rushed to the tent after the accident. And he'd probably witnessed every incriminating moment!

Odd how everything kept coming back to Waite. Oh, sure, she worried about J.B.—she could definitely do without him wondering about "Della's" strange behavior until Erin could finally get out of here—but it occurred to Erin that she was more emotionally off-balance in the presence of Della's former lover than she was in the company of the woman's husband. Would she have cared one whit about that scene at the dinner party last night if Waite had not been present? And why was she going to such pains to avoid eye contact with the man? Why were her dreams filled with erotic images of him?

Simple chemistry...mere attraction. Her brain suggested that was the reason, but her heart wasn't buying it. Besides the eerie connection she felt, there was more to Waite MacKinnon than a very masculine physique and gorgeous face. He was a fine, honorable man. He'd slipped up and kissed her yesterday at the creek, but his violent reaction to the mistake, the way he'd gathered his loyalty to his friend around himself like some sort of invisible shield—it spoke of an innate decency that was appealing to Erin.

Much too appealing.

"Excuse me." Erin's green eyes locked with the black ones of the man her thoughts had been centered on. He stood next to her, suspicion in his gaze and impatience in his stance. Oh, Lord, *appealing* didn't seem quite strong enough a word to describe him. He was so tall...so daunting...so capable of causing her untold trouble.

"I need to get to my seat, Della."

Erin didn't want to let him pass. She didn't want him anywhere near J.B., but she pulled in her knees anyway, albeit slowly. She swallowed, watching Waite out of the corner of her eye as he sat down next to J.B. and wondering just what he would say to his partner. He turned to look at her, and she knew by his expression that he'd seen all of it. Wonderful. Just what she needed. *J.B., you should have seen what I just saw!* She pulled her gaze from his, concentrating instead on the arena where Will Rogers was being introduced by George Miller.

"The boy all right?" J.B. asked.

"Miraculously enough, he is," Waite answered.

"Get the wind knocked out of him?"

"Oh, more than that."

Erin clenched her fists. *Come on, Waite, don't pick now to drop the strong,* silent *image.*

"You don't say? Well, Doc Kenner's been known to perform a few miracles in his time."

"True. But he had some help this time."

Erin swallowed. Hard. She couldn't help it, she had to look at them. J.B. had lifted a brow at Waite. "What do you mean?" he asked.

Erin grabbed J.B.'s arm and pointed at the arena. "Have you ever seen anyone like that Will Rogers? He can do just about anything with a rope, can't he? Mr. Wyndham," she said, snagging the banker's attention, "what do you think? Is Will amazing or what?"

The man smiled and nodded. "Quite astounding."

"Astounding. That's the word for him, all right," she rattled on. "And he's a native Oklahoman, of course. J.B., have you told Mr. Wyndham about all our famous native sons? I'm sure he'd be interested to hear about them. And the outlaws. The whole state was a huge outlaw hideout at one time, you know." Her father's pride in his state came in handy. Erin knew Oklahoma's history as well as any non-native could. "Make sure J.B. tells you all about the outlaws."

"*TULSA WORLD*, MR. MUNRO!" the young man shouted as he sprinted toward them. He held up a camera. "Can I get a picture of you and Mr. Rogers for the paper, sir?"

Erin held in a groan. *Aw, come on,* she thought, *can't we just go home?* She'd loved the show, had nearly embarrassed J.B. to death by gaping like an idiot when Will Rogers and Tom Mix had come over to talk to their old friends, the Munros, but her nerves were shot. It was bad enough that Waite kept giving her those I-saw-what-you-did-and-I-want-to-know-how-you-did-it looks, but Erin had also remembered that she wasn't safe in this crowd of people. It was altogether possible that Della's murderer enjoyed Wild West shows. How she'd slipped up and forgotten that fact, she didn't know. What she did know was that being a target did not sit any better with her than the possibility of Waite telling J.B. what he'd seen.

"Well, certainly, son. Della, I want you in the picture, as well, dear," J.B. said, gathering her to his side.

"Oh, J.B., no. Really, I must look...a fright," she objected, pulling away. She gestured toward the Packard. "I'll just wait in the car. I don't like having my picture taken."

Waite and J.B. both stared at her as though she'd grown another head. Too late, the tour guide from the future's words drifted in. *It was said that Mrs. Munro loved to have her picture taken....* Oh, great. She'd slipped up again.

"I'd believe that of almost anyone but Della," Waite said to J.B. with a chuckle. He shot her a challenging look, but kept his tone light. "What do you think, J.B., has someone replaced Della with an impostor?"

Erin glared at him. Waite MacKinnon was playing with her now, jerking her chain. He knew somehow—had probably heard her ask Miller not to tell J.B.—that she'd rather not face questions from J.B. about saving the cowboy's life. Why wouldn't he just mind his own business?

Della Munro, and therefore Erin, was none of his business. He'd made that point loud and clear. So why wasn't he following his own stupid dictum? No, not stupid, Erin told herself. Smart. Sensible. A dictum to live by.

She'd had it up to here with Mr. Waite MacKinnon and all his thunderous looks. There hadn't been one thing she'd done today to merit his glares and frowns. He'd told her to stay the hell away from him and she had. She hadn't so much as spoken to the man! Now here he was, putting her on the spot. And seeming to enjoy it.

She fluffed her hair, smiling and giving Waite a flirtatious wink as she moved back to stand beside

J.B. "Oh, you know me so well, don't you, Waite? I was just hoping for a little attention, as always. You men haven't paid me nearly enough today, what with all these distractions going on. Can you blame a girl for wanting to be...persuaded?" *There you go, Waite. Is that* Della *enough for you?*

She linked arms with J.B. and Will Rogers, then fluttered her lashes at the photographer, laying it on even thicker. "Will this be a flattering pose?"

The flash went off, and Erin shot Waite an are-you-satisfied-now? look. But it didn't seem to be enough for him. He didn't glare at her again, but his bemused expression disturbed her even more.

Wyndham sidled up next to Will Rogers as their group began to disperse, pulling a 101 program from his front pocket. "Would you honor me with an autograph, Mr. Rogers?"

Erin shifted her attention from Waite to the two men—the Boston banker and Oklahoma's favorite son—and wondered why the heck she was worried about Waite MacKinnon's facial expressions when she was standing next to Will Rogers. Incredible! God, what an incredible day! Just how many people her age—she pictured herself telling her grandchildren someday—can say they saw the *real* Will Rogers Follies?

"It's an honor being asked," Rogers said with a boyish, crinkle-eyed smile. His lasso was still looped over one arm, and the battered cowboy hat Erin had seen in so many pictures of the man was tilted back off his forehead. "That Boston I hear in your voice?" he asked, scribbling his name.

"Yes, it is," Wyndham replied, clearly impressed.

Erin caught J.B. giving Rogers a covert wink. "My friend Wyndham, here, is a banker, Will."

Rogers chuckled. "You don't say. My daddy was a banker, you know," he told Wyndham. "Wanted me to be one in the worst way."

This seemed to tickle Wyndham to death. His smile broadened. "I didn't know that! You almost became a banker?"

"Oh, now, I didn't say that." He handed the program back to the man with a self-deprecating grin. "As a banker, Mr. Wyndham, I would have made a damned good roper."

He laughed right along with the rest of them, then shook hands all around. Erin probably held on to his hand just a moment longer than she should have, but couldn't help herself. History, she thought, marveling again that she had actually met Will Rogers.

Then the four of them, Wyndham, J.B., Waite and herself, climbed into the Packard for the return trip to the mansion, and Erin leaned back in the luxurious seat. Exhausted, she closed her eyes.

The sensation that her seatmate was studying her was strong, and though she tried to ignore it, after a few more miles, she couldn't stand it another minute. She opened her eyes, locking gazes with him. "You told me to stay the hell away from you," she said quietly enough that the comment went unheard by the men in the front seat, who were caught up in their own conversation. "So take your own advice and do the same."

He looked angry with himself, then turned away from her. "I did say that, didn't I?"

"Yes, you did."

"I wonder why that's become so hard to do," he muttered to his window.

FRANKLIN THOMAS SPLASHED cold water on his newly clean-shaven jaw, then shut off the faucet and reached for the towel the hotel provided. Glancing up at the mirror, he almost cried out in alarm.

Without the beard, it was his brother's face he saw, not his own. *Henry,* he thought, grief slicing through his gut. *Henry, will I always see you when I pass a mirror now?*

The water dripped from his chin like tears, and he quickly blotted them, then tossed away the towel. Too many tears had been shed. By his mother, his sister, everyone who had loved Henry.

Franklin hadn't cried. And he hadn't questioned God as everyone else had. Because he'd stopped believing in God when Henry had died.

God in his mercy... God in his mercy...

Franklin remembered the priest's words at Henry's funeral. Over and over the man had chanted the words, lying...lying...lying. Rage had flooded Franklin's veins and he'd wanted to scream, had wanted to shake the mourners who sat nodding their heads, accepting the lie. He'd wanted to shout at them, *Look at this young man, my brother, who only wanted to serve your benevolent Father, and tell me of your God's "mercy"... his "tolerance" and "forgiveness."*

But he hadn't. He'd only kissed his grieving mother and sister goodbye, then left to find the woman responsible and mete out justice in a way that Henry's God would approve of.

An eye for an eye and a tooth for a tooth. Franklin gave a cynical laugh as he put on his suit coat and left the Tulsa hotel room, thinking there were select tenets in the Gospel he agreed with wholeheartedly.

He pushed thoughts of his beloved brother aside, concentrating on where he would go next. His plan was to get out of Oklahoma, but not so quickly that it appeared he was fleeing. Justice had been served, and Franklin didn't care so much that he might have to pay for his sin, he just didn't want his family to suffer anymore. They had suffered enough.

He bought a paper from a boy hawking them on the sidewalk outside the hotel, then hailed a taxi.

"Where to?" the cabbie asked.

Franklin climbed into the back seat. "Train station."

The taxi had pulled up to the station when Franklin saw the picture of Della Munro.

"Here ya go, mister. Train station."

A mistake. It had to be a mistake! But the caption said otherwise. The picture had been taken yesterday at the 101 Ranch.

The fevered rage that had left him after he avenged his brother's death returned, dragging with it the hatred, and the pain. A sob rose in his throat, but he forced it back. He'd killed her, goddamn it, killed her with his own hands! She'd been dead when he'd left her on the floor of that cave!

"Mister? Said we're here...."

The voice broke into Franklin's frantic thoughts. He looked up, saw the impatience in the driver's expression. "I—" He glanced out the window, noting the crowds of people streaming in and out of the station "Yes... H-how much do I owe you?"

"You okay?"

Franklin slapped the paper closed and dug into his pocket for money. He was certain his face was as pale as parchment. "I'm...fine. Here," he said, handing the man a fistful of money and stumbling out of the cab, newspaper in hand.

Dead, he thought again after purchasing a ticket back to Munro. He could have sworn the bitch had been dead.

WAITE SHOOK HIS HEAD, declining the servant's offer of a cocktail. Though the hour was late, the party J.B. had thrown for Harrison Wyndham's last night in town was still in full swing. The guest list was made up of oil barons, ranchers, state and city politicians and their wives. The cream of Munro society, all dressed in their finery and cele- brating. The celebratory mood was due to J.B. and Waite's successful wooing of the Boston banker. Triumphant smiles and hearty handshakes told the story. The man was as impressed as hell with J. B. Munro's Oklahoma, and he hadn't been subtle in relaying that to all the businessmen in attendance.

Edgy and annoyed by the loud music, Waite moved to the wall of glass that overlooked the back of the estate. He slid his hands into his pockets to stifle the urge to check his pocket watch again. He was J.B.'s partner. So why wasn't he as thrilled as J.B. and the others at the prospect of more pros- perity? Why, lately, had his success begun to feel pointless?

There had been a time when pride in his accomplishments had meant everything, when he had wanted to show the world that he was something... someone.

But was it really the world he'd been out to prove himself to? Or just one woman? Or one woman and her husband—Della and J.B.

He couldn't remember ever making a conscious decision to give up the goal of owning his own ranch, but he did recall the drive and ambition he'd been fired with to move all the way to the top of Munro Rail Lines after J.B. had married Della. *Later,* he'd told himself. *After I've made it here, I'll have my dream.* His partner had told him several times through the years that he'd done Waite a favor by marrying Della. She would have ruined Waite. She was a scheming, deceitful woman, and J.B. had known Waite would never have become the success he was with her as an emotional albatross. Waite hadn't been so naive he'd believed that was J.B.'s sole motivation, but he'd come to believe J.B. had been right.

But Waite hadn't been insightful enough to understand why he'd remained with Munro Rail Lines all these years, had he? The light suddenly dawning, Waite shook his head. It hadn't been the world he'd been fighting to prove himself to; it had been them. She had rejected him, and his pride had been torn to shreds; J.B. had thought he wasn't man enough to "handle" Della. But he'd shown them both. He had come out on top. A successful man.

J.B. approached him just then, clapping him on the shoulder. "Seems Wyndham wants to discuss business, Waite," he said, his eyes gleaming. "In my office."

"Congratulations, J.B. It worked out just as you'd planned."

"Usually does."

"Yes, it does, doesn't it?"

"You'll want to be in on this. After all, you got the ball rolling."

Waite looked away, gazing out at the velvet night, the ebony sky strewn with stars. Not diamonds or twinkling jewels, as J.B. liked to describe them to visiting luminaries. Just stars.

"Not this time, J.B.," he said in a quiet voice.

"Something wrong, son? You deserve as much credit for convincing Wyndham as I do. I don't think now is the time for that country-boy modesty."

Waite met his gaze, irritated by the condescending edge in his partner's tone. "I'm not trying to be modest, J.B. I just...need to think some things over. Going to turn in early tonight."

Wyndham appeared at their side, a fat cigar in one hand, a cocktail in the other and a cowboy hat on his head. His eyes were bright from the liquor he'd imbibed all evening, but Waite knew the man wasn't intoxicated on alcohol alone. He recognized the expression on the banker's face; he'd seen it so many times in his own mirror. There was no mistaking the look of a man satisfied that he was about to make a killing.

"Munro?" he said, looking altogether ridiculous in the Stetson George Miller had given him. "I'm anxious to make some plans."

"I like the sound of that, Harrison." J.B. gave Waite another concerned look before leaving with the banker.

J.B. would want an explanation in the morning, but Waite really didn't care at the moment. It was frightening, in fact, just how much he didn't care.

As he caught sight of Della out of the corner of his eye, Waite's apathy disappeared. He watched her peer after her husband and the banker until they had left the room. Then she made excuses to the oilman's wife she'd been talking with, and wove her way through the crowd to a set of doors that led outside.

If there was a woman on earth Waite should despise, it was her. But as long as he was facing truths tonight, he might as well own up to another one. Damn it, she made him feel. Too much. Eight years ago, she'd been the woman he'd wanted beside him forever; then she'd shattered his soul. He'd thought he had drummed her out of his mind and his heart all these years since. He frowned. He had. He hadn't wanted a thing to do with her again.

Then she'd come out of the tunnels that night. And ever since then, he'd wanted her again.

Why?

ERIN STRUCK OUT for the guesthouse, feeling like some sort of commando on a night mission. She had purposely worn a black sheath to the party tonight, not wishing to be spotted outside. If there was a door to the tunnels in the guesthouse, and she was certain the tour guide had said there was, then she would find it. She just wished she could have broken away last night as she'd planned, but J.B. had kept a close eye on her.

Ducking behind a row of hedges, she quickened her pace. J.B. and Wyndham's little meeting might last for hours...or only minutes. Since Erin had no way of knowing, time was of the essence.

The hedge ended several yards in front of the guesthouse door, so Erin glanced about for signs of servants, then peered up at J.B.'s office window, which overlooked this side of the grounds. Good. The curtains were drawn. Feeling reasonably certain she wouldn't be seen, she sprinted the distance, hoping like hell the thin letter opener in her clutch purse would do the trick if the door was locked.

Which it was. Erin sweated it out for several anxiety-ridden moments, jiggling the letter opener this way and that, sending up prayers and mumbling curses. The lock finally clicked open and she closed her eyes and sighed with relief, then slipped inside.

She peered out the window, checking J.B.'s office again to make sure the curtains were still closed before switching on a small table lamp. She blinked, her eyes adjusting to the sudden brightness, then gasped. Erin had known, of course, that this was the room where she had first seen J.B. in 1994, but it chilled her to see it again. She wasted no time in finding the door she felt sure led to the tunnel. It was located between the living room and a bedroom, and was similar to the one in the fireplace—industrial gray, made of heavy steel. There was no padlock on this door, but it was locked all the same. And this time Erin's letter opener didn't work.

She paced back to the living room. *Okay,* she

thought, and glanced around the room, a fingertip at her temple. *If I were hiding a key to that lock, where in this room would I put it?*

CHAPTER ELEVEN

WAITE STARED AT THE guesthouse door after it closed behind her, not proud of the licentious thoughts slinking through his head.

Walk away. Just walk the hell away from here...from her. You don't want to know why you want her. Why she's changed. You just want her.

But in his mind, he tumbled back in time, remembering their clandestine meetings when she had sneaked away from J.B.—her guardian at the time—to be with him.

Remembering. Remembering. Remembering.

Young. They'd been so young. Her hair had been long then, and had felt like warm silk in his hands, the auburn strands forever catching the light.

Sunlight...lamplight...candlelight... And he'd been unable to resist holding it in his fingers, draping it over his body. He remembered its warmth. His clearest recollection of their time together was of his constant need for warmth in his life.

And he'd thought he'd found it in her. Looking past her cool persona out of bed to the heat they generated in it, his inexperienced heart had decided she was his future.

But she'd wanted J.B., and Waite had learned his lesson well. With every woman since, he'd known not to mistake the carnal or the prurient for love.

Cold... Uncaring... But the woman who had just switched on the light in the guesthouse was neither of those things. She was different now. How was that possible? He'd watched her save a stranger's life, pouring her breath into him and shedding quiet tears of relief when he lived. And the day before, when Waite had kissed her, when he had thought to prove to her and to himself that she was the same conniving bitch she'd always been, she had apologized for the pain she'd inflicted. Was such a remarkable transformation possible? She'd said the bump on the head had made her see how wrong she'd been, but Waite had thought her apology was just another ploy. Was he wrong?

He pictured her eyes again, the way they seemed a darker green than before, and thought of the things she'd said she had "forgotten." His mind swirled with images and the heady sensations he'd felt when he'd held her in his arms beside that creek—her taste, the feel of her slender body molded to his. And for one insane moment Waite actually entertained the theory that she *wasn't*

Della. Then he shook his head and almost laughed aloud. *Insane* was the word for it.

He approached the guesthouse quietly, deciding he wanted—no, needed—answers after all. He opened the door, but didn't move immediately into the room. He simply stared at her in silence. She had stacked pieces of his empty luggage next to the tall bookshelves that lined one wall and was climbing the tower of baggage. As he watched, she held on to a high shelf with one hand while reaching to the top shelf with the other. Waite watched quietly for a few seconds more as she extracted the books, one by one, felt around in the space behind, then replaced them.

"Just what the hell is it you're looking for?"

She shrieked, and lost her footing on the cases. Before Waite could get to her, she tumbled to the floor, pulling a few of the books—heavy ones—down with her.

"For God's sake, Della." He lifted the book that covered her face. She groaned. The damned cut on her forehead was open again.

"This thing is never going to heal," he muttered, whipping out his handkerchief and pressing it to the wound.

She swatted at his hands and sat up. Yanking the handkerchief away from him, she said, "Well, it might have a chance if you'd quit sneaking up on me and shouting all the time. This is the second time you've done that, you know. And it's not the cut I'm worried about. I think I've sprained my ankle."

She reached for it, but Waite pressed a hand to her shoulder. "Sit still. I'll look at it." He turned and reached for the ankle, not able to avoid looking at the silk-covered length of leg that led to it. He'd told himself he hadn't noticed her legs earlier at the party, but he'd been lying. He'd noticed. God, how he'd noticed.

He picked up the heavy tome that had landed on her ankle, then slid the black sequined high-heeled shoe off her foot. Already it had started to swell. He touched it.

"Ow!"

He glanced over his shoulder at her. "I guess asking you to stand on it would be out of the question."

Her eyes were closed, her mouth pinched, her head thrown back. "Crap," she said through gritted teeth, then opened her eyes again. "I'll bet it's sprained at the very least."

"Well, you can't just sit here all night. I'll move you to the—"

"Waite, watch out!"

His gaze followed hers to the bookshelf as she glanced up. Another big book was teetering on the edge, threatening to catch him right on the head. Waite reached up to grab it, but she shoved at his shoulders with both hands, knocking him aside and warning, "It's going to hit you!"

She shouted in pain when the book hit her instead, landing square on her injured ankle.

"Damn it, I could've caught it!" He picked up the book and flung it away.

"Ouch!"

"Well, what did you expect?" His gaze sharpened and he shook his head at her. "Why the hell did you do that?"

"Instinct," she mumbled.

"You instinctively want to be hurt?" He lifted her in his arms, stunned by the immediate reaction he felt to touching her. "This ought to be just the thing, then," he said sarcastically, not liking his body's instant response to holding her.

She grimaced, but didn't say a word.

"Sorry," he muttered, and tried not to jostle the ankle as he carried her through the guesthouse to its only bedroom. Setting her on top of the bed he'd slept in—the one he'd *lost* sleep in because of her— he reached for one of the pillows and propped her foot on it. Then he found the bedside lamp, turning it on and casting the room in a rosy glow.

He sat down on the bed, his thigh all too near hers. She hiked up the gown and bent at the waist, craning her neck to see the ankle. Her gaze lifted and connected with his. "The stockings...uh, they make it impossible to tell anything."

"Yes."

It amused him to see the color rise in her cheeks. Another novelty.

She glanced down again. Waite couldn't look away from the sight of her hand snaking under the gown to unfasten her garter, then roll down the stocking and take it off.

Waite's throat went dry. With his hand, he circled her ankle, intent on gauging the extent of her injury, but unable to concentrate because of the myriad emotions fighting for control inside him.

He had scolded her for pushing him aside when the book pitched off the shelf, but in truth what she had done was as selfless and caring as what he'd witnessed at the 101 Ranch. That type of behavior from this woman confused the hell out of him. He tried to think of the day she'd told him she'd used him to get to J.B. Tried to remember her very words, her face, the ice in her gaze...but he couldn't conjure up those pictures. They were hazy, yellowed at the edges...like old photographs. Waite could only see her clearly as she'd looked after he'd kissed her at the creek, trembling as she clasped her shirt in her fist, telling him not to call her Della.

And he felt the same heat of arousal he'd felt then. He felt her clinging to him, touching him.

"Waite..."

Her voice was low and whispery, and he suddenly realized he was no longer ministering to an injury, but was stroking her satiny skin with his thumbs. He lifted his head and saw immediately that she knew what was going on inside him. Her feelings were just as transparent. The look in her eyes told of longing...desire.... She scooted toward him on the bed and rested her hand on his thigh. "I want you, too. I feel as if I've wanted you forever. It's crazy, but—"

"But it's not right," he said, his jaw set, his gut tight. "You're not mine."

"But...I have the feeling it would be more right than anything I've ever done. I...I just know." She slid her hand higher on his leg. Lifting her other hand to his jaw, she stroked his skin as he had hers.

Blood pounded through his veins and his body hardened. *Not mine to take,* he thought, even as he turned to press his mouth against her palm.

He heard her breath quicken and remembered the glorious taste of her mouth two days ago. The kiss that never should have been. "Della..." he said, his voice raw.

"No. Please." She obliterated the distance between them, sealing their mouths together and wrapping her arms around him. Waite groaned and lowered her to the bed. "Don't call me that. I can't bear it."

He rose up, giving her a sharp look that conveyed uneasiness, and Erin could have kicked herself for what she'd said. She brought him back to her, angled her mouth over his, boldly sweeping her tongue over his lips and then inside. *Don't think,* she pleaded silently. *Don't think. Just . . . love me.*

He touched her breast, and Erin groaned. Drowning in his kiss, she forgot everything else, felt nothing but his mouth, the thunderous beat of his heart next to hers.

Her hands slid inside his jacket, and she tugged at the stiff fabric of his shirt until it came free of his pants. His skin beneath it was hot, firm, and deliciously hard to the sensitive pads of her fingertips. He scrambled to get out of his jacket and then the shirt, tossing them both across the bed.

Erin drank in the sight of his bare chest. She'd touched but hadn't had the chance to look. She raised herself up to work at the fastenings at the back of her gown, wanting to feel his muscled, bare skin against hers.

"No," he said, plucking her hands away. "Let me do it."

He made quick work of it, then brushed the silky fabric from her shoulders. It pooled at her waist.

The brassiere she wore would have been frowned at by a man from her time. It was black, but not lacy or sexy, low-cut or alluring. Though it was stiff and utilitarian by modern standards, it lit a fire in Waite's eyes. Erin didn't know why exactly that gave her such a thrill; she only knew that the way he looked at her made desire surge through her bloodstream, creating an aching need.

Waite intensified the ache. Clasping her shoulders in his strong hands, he lowered his head until his lips and tongue glided along the tops of her breasts. Erin urgently laced her fingers through his hair, holding his dark head close as he licked and sucked her exposed flesh. When his mouth moved lower and he kissed her through the bra, Erin caught her breath. She fumbled for the catch in the back. He shook his head, mumbling something Erin couldn't make out, then delivered torturous caresses through the cloth, rubbing, stroking, kissing her until she thought madness was certainly close at hand.

"Waite...please."

Giving in to her plea, he reached around, unclasped the bra and drew it off her. Then he pulled her into his arms, pressing her bare breasts to his chest as his mouth locked onto hers again.

Erin discovered that she could willingly let go of the rest of the world for passion. The knowledge shook her a bit, but she didn't allow it to stop her from pouring herself into the kiss...giving him everything she was, everything she wanted to give him.

"God..." he whispered against her skin, the fever in his blood at the boiling point. He hauled her closer. His hands on her hips, he pressed her tight against his arousal, wanting, needing, to be inside her.

Guilt should have cut him to shreds, but oddly, he hadn't felt its piercing edge.

Mine. It was the only thought in his head as his lips captured her earlobe, his tongue washing it as his hands skimmed down to her breasts again. "You're mine tonight."

Her palms bracketed his face and she nodded. "That makes you mine, as well. But not just for tonight. I know there's more because I saw you...before I came here...."

He rose up to look at her. "What—?"

"No. Not now. Don't ask now." Then she was kissing him again, stealing the question from his lips just as surely as she stole his breath away when she reached for the buttons of his trousers. Impossibly, his arousal strengthened. Her fingers brushed over him, and he knew he was close to losing all control.

He pushed her hands away and shucked off his trousers, his shoes and his socks, then came back to her. "Do you know what you're doing to me?" he asked, removing her gown completely and pitching it on top of his discarded clothing. His hands slid up her legs, blazing a trail for the mouth that followed in their wake, stringing hot, erotic kisses over her skin.

"Yes. God, yes. Because you're doing the same to me. Oh, Waite..." She fell backward when his tongue moistened the skin around and beneath her garter. She felt him unfasten it, sweep the silk down, then quickly dispatch the rest of her undergarments until there was nothing between them but her secrets and some seventy-odd years.

He moved up from her thigh, and Erin gasped when she felt his intimate kiss. Slowly she began to unravel—her heart, nerves, her very soul—as he laved her most sensitive place with his tongue. Sending up silent prayers, she trembled under his ministrations, struggled toward release.

It shattered her when it finally came, and she sobbed his name aloud, gripping his shoulders as she shuddered again and again with the powerful orgasm.

He climbed her body, fusing her mouth with his, his hands kneading her hair. "Sweet...so sweet to hear my name on your lips again...like this..."

"Not again, Waite. This is the first time for us."
He went still, but Erin gave him no time for questions. She reached down between them, stroked his hard length with her fingers. "Come inside, Waite. For the first time."

Her touch set him on fire, obliterating the need to know the meaning of her cryptic remark, and he slipped inside her. Slowly at first, as though time were their personal possession, he moved within her, tasting impatience on her lips, urgency in her movements. Still he paced his thrusts, wanting to prolong the intimacy, feeling truly alive for the first time in years.

But need outpaced him. Her hands were all over him—his shoulders, the small of his back, his thighs—racing, skimming, prodding, pushing him toward the final crest. Holding her gaze with his, her hair still tangled in his hands, he saw how close she was to release. With every ounce of fortitude he had, Waite held his own pleasure back, urging her to the peak. And when she cried out, he withdrew from her body, using every ounce of self-control to avoid the risk of making her pregnant. Then, tightening their embrace, listening to her soft, soughing breath at his ear and feeling her body cradle the length of him as it had when he'd been inside, he found his own release.

They had made love before...but this was different. Then it had been carnal, almost impersonal. He'd offered her his heart, but she had refused to accept anything other than his body. But this time...

He rose up on his elbows, and gently brushed his thumbs over her closed eyelids. His throat tight with emotion, he searched his soul for the guilt that should have been there, but stumbled into another emotion—love.

I love her...again, he thought, stunned by the realization.

ERIN'S EYES FLUTTERED open, and guilt flooded in. He would have walked away—if she hadn't pushed him into it, sanctioned it, told him it was right for her.... She swallowed and lowered her gaze.

He caught her chin with two fingers and nudged her to look at him again. "Don't, Della. No regrets. For some strange reason, I'm not sorry right now that we did this. I probably will be with the morning light, but—"

"No!" Her denial was powerful, strident. "Just...trust me on this one. You have no reason to feel sorry or guilty. No reason at all."

His brows drew together over confused black eyes, and Erin wanted to grab hold of him and never let go. She wanted to keep him within her heart, within her grasp, forever.

"You can't shoulder the entire responsibility for this. I wanted you.... God, how I wanted you."

And I wanted you, she thought. *Too much.*

She still did... and always would. Pain gripped her heart. She'd never known it would hurt so much to lose a love, because she'd never truly felt this way before. And never would again, she thought sadly.

"I... shouldn't have followed you here...." Waite's mouth tightened, and he rolled onto his back. She knew he was thinking about J.B.—his partner, his friend—and was torturing himself for no reason.

"You didn't betray him," she said quietly, and he turned to look at her again. She laced her fingers with his and brought them to her mouth for a soft kiss. "I'm not her, Waite. I'm not his wife."

CHAPTER TWELVE

"DAMN IT, DELLA!" He sprang up, flinging her hand away, then moved quickly toward their clothes. "Here. Get dressed."

"It's true, Waite. I'm not her. Don't tell me you haven't wondered about it sometimes, because I've seen how suspicious you've been of me. I know you've—"

"I said, get dressed, Della."

He had gone from blistering passion to sweet affection and now to cold anger. Erin wanted to cry. She scrambled over to him, wincing at the pain in her ankle. "No! Listen to me, Waite. Tell me you haven't noticed some of the differences. Tell me you didn't question what I did for that cowboy at the 101. How could Della have known about that?"

"You said you heard a doctor describing it . . . at a party."

"Well, I lied."

He narrowed his eyes at her, then turned his back, shrugging into his shirt. "I know you did. You've never been to Europe with J.B."

"I haven't? Oh. Well, there. You see? I'm not her and you know it!" God, it felt good getting this off her chest. Better than she had expected. And she couldn't continue the charade with Waite any longer. Not after what they had just shared. She simply couldn't abide lying to him anymore. And she wouldn't allow him to be eaten up with guilt for something he hadn't done.

"No." He dragged his slacks up muscular legs, then fastened the buttons at his fly. "What I know is that I *wanted* to believe you weren't you. I wanted it because, for the past two days, I've wanted to sleep with you again. So I convinced myself of it for about two seconds outside this guesthouse. But that's crazy, Della. We both know that's crazy."

Erin smiled at the way doubt had crept into his words. "Okay," she said. "Explain how I know CPR."

"CP what?"

"Cardiopulmonary resuscitation. CPR. What I performed on the cowboy at the 101. Della wouldn't know how to do it—Della or anyone else from this time period couldn't know. Because it won't come into being until sometime in the 1960s."

His expression went flat, his dark eyes considering her with a look Erin interpreted easily: *She's lost her mind.* "Time period?" he repeated tentatively.

Hadn't she known she would get this reaction if she told anyone living in 1925? "I know it sounds crazy, Waite. Impossible. Don't you think I've thought the same thing? But it's true. Della is dead. I saw her murdered in the tunnel by a man with a beard."

"Murdered—"

His eyes widened, and Erin hurried on. "The locket . . . it somehow brought me back to this time from mine. I don't know how, of course, but I know that the locket was somehow responsible. That and the portrait of Della. I touched it and my locket at the same time, and bang! I wound up here. Don't you see? That's why I've been so crazy to get my locket back . . . so I can go home. It's my ticket home."

He shook his head, clearly stunned, then lowered himself to the edge of the bed. "And home is . . . another time? The 1960s?"

"Nineties. The 1990s. You don't believe a word of this, do you?"

He stared at her for a long moment. "I believe that you're either lying again—but why you would create such a convoluted, unbelievable tale I'll never know—or that fall in the tunnel caused more damage than a simple case of amnesia."

"I made that up."

"The fall."

"No, the amnesia. Because I kept slipping up, Waite. I couldn't answer questions about Della's past because I didn't know her past. But until I got the locket back, I couldn't risk anyone finding out I *wasn't* Della."

"Because . . . ?"

"Because J.B. would ship me to an asylum, that's why. He threatened to do that because I went into the tunnels with another man—the man who must have murdered the real Della. It seems Della has been pushing J.B. for years and he's just about had enough of her. I guess locking her up in a padded room would solve all his problems with her. What do you think he'd do if I tried to convince him I wasn't his wife? He'd have all the evidence he needed for the commitment papers, wouldn't he? And then where would I be? Even farther from my locket, right?"

Waite put his head in his hands and sighed loudly. "Oh, God, Della."

"No." She moved next to him on the bed, peeling his hands away from his face. "Erin. Erin Sawyer." She touched his face, turning it toward hers, then kissed him . . . softly, gently.

"I've never been married to J.B., and I was not your lover all those years ago, Waite. You didn't betray your friend and business partner tonight.

And I won't let you feel guilty about it when it just isn't true."

His lips were cold at first, unmoving. But Erin didn't give up easily. She attacked his disbelief, his hesitancy, by pouring every ounce of love she had for the man into her kiss. Ignoring the pain in her ankle, she scooted into his lap, then wrapped her arms around his neck.

"Waite..." she whispered against his mouth, his cheek, his nose, then his mouth again. "I couldn't let you continue to believe I'm her. I don't know why I'm here...why I look so much like a woman I'd never known about...or even why I witnessed her murder. But I do know one thing. It's the only thing, in fact, that I'm certain about right now."

"Wh-what?"

Erin took great pleasure in his stutter. She also took pleasure in the rapid beating of his heart as she touched him...caressed his awakening arousal against her thigh.

"I know that since the moment I first saw you at the party, I've been knocked out by you. Attracted, compelled, smitten, lovesick—whatever you want to call it." She stroked his cheek, smiling. "There's something between us...something good, Waite. Something I think you feel, too," she whispered. "Good, not immoral. If you can believe nothing else, believe in that." She kissed his bottom lip, then tugged it inside her mouth.

A low groan issued from his throat, and he pulled her hard against his chest, taking her down with him to the bed again. The kiss was wild and unruly; all animal lust and excitement. Erin gloried in it, grasping fistfuls of his hair, pressing into him as though she could never get close enough . . . and could never let him get away. She tried to ignore the pang of sorrow that hit her at that last thought. She'd asked him to believe in what they felt for each other, but it was all so temporary. Fleeting . . . impermanent. A single moment out of time.

Waite tore off his clothes again, and, bracing himself above her, he joined their bodies a second time. But instead of the pleasure she'd hoped to see, there was agony in his expression. It tore at her heart. Tears, not of joy but of grief, gathered in her eyes.

"I'm . . . sorry," Waite whispered into her hair when it was over. He rose up on his elbows, gazing down at her for a moment before shaking his head sadly. "Oh, God. I want to believe you're someone else. You don't know how much, but—"

"It's enough," she said, and blinked back more tears. It was all she had, for now.

THEY HAD FALLEN ASLEEP in each other's arms.
Erin didn't know what had woken her, but she did
know she couldn't stay wrapped in Waite's warmth
all night, however much she wished she could.

Carefully extricating herself from his embrace,
she left the bed, glancing one last time at the man
as he slept.

Oh, Lord, he was gorgeous, and even more so in
repose. There was a vulnerability in his features not
present during waking hours. It reminded her of
what they had talked about after the second time
they had made love.

She had wanted to know about him, about his
life before J.B. and becoming a tycoon. He'd
frowned that disbelieving frown again, but hu-
mored her nevertheless. He seemed awkward at
first, then he relaxed as he proceeded to tell her of
his time at the 101, how he had come to be there,
his childhood, and finally, the deaths of his mother
and father.

Waite hadn't asked about Erin's past, but she'd
told him anyway, even though he'd found it difficult to comprehend much of what she described.
He let her go on about the changes that would
happen to the world, scowling slightly at things like
televisions in every home, men traveling to the
moon and computers that would virtually take over
the business world and more.

She sighed and tiptoed over to her clothes. Slipping back into the gown, she grabbed up her stockings and garter belt, knowing they couldn't risk being caught by J.B. Waite was still convinced Erin was Della, despite what she had told him. If confronted by his friend, Waite wouldn't defend himself with Erin's explanation. She didn't want to be responsible for a rift in their friendship.

She glanced back over her shoulder at the man who had come to mean so much to her in such a short time. The pain of knowing she would have to leave him cut cruelly into her gut, and she held back a sob as she left the bedroom.

From the front window of the guesthouse, Erin could see that it was still dark outside but knew it wouldn't be long before the sun came up. She moved as quickly as her ankle would permit. In the living room, she nearly tripped over the journal that had fallen with the rest of the books last night. She almost pitched it aside. But something compelled her to open the journal and examine the pretty handwriting.

"This diary belongs to Della Richards," Erin read, "a gift from Jonathan Bartholomew Munro. 1909."

Midway down the page was the first entry in the book.

"I am ten years old today, Diary, and you are my birthday gift from my new mama and papa."

EDITH, THE UPSTAIRS MAID, headed for her room, careful to keep her footsteps silent. She'd be damned if she'd listen to old Simmons, with his snooty, condescending air. All these new rules the butler had come up with were ridiculous, if you asked her. Especially now that he'd said she could no longer come and go as she pleased after hours.

Used to be if she had a hankering for a late snack, she'd just tramp up from the servants' quarters to the kitchen and take what she wanted. No harm there. All that leftover food would've gone to waste anyway.

Tightfisted old bastard. "You're fed well enough," he'd said with his nose in the air when Edith had complained. "Be glad for what you get."

Glad for what you get. Ha! Bad enough that she slaved away in this immoral household. She wasn't going to put up with these stupid new rules, too. No sirree.

When she topped the stairs, a noise sent her scurrying into a corner next to a window. For several anxious moments, she strained to hear it again. Must have been her imagination, she thought, and began to move away from the window. But then she spotted something outside, someone sneaking around out there. Edith squinted, noting that he or she was moving toward the mansion from the direction of the guesthouse.

"Well, what do you know about that?" Edith said under her breath when finally she could make out who the person was. "Miss Della, coming from the guesthouse where Waite MacKinnon stays." She grinned broadly when she saw the stockings and garter belt in Della's hands.

"My, my, my. What will Mr. Munro have to say about this?"

She thought for a moment about Simmons and his rule about staying in the servants' quarters after hours. Would Munro let his butler fire Edith, even though she was doing the man a service by telling him about his cheating whore of a wife?

It would be worth it, she decided, to see that no-account floozy get her just deserts. Edith had thought Della Munro would never be allowed back in the house after what happened four years ago. Pregnant by a man other than her husband, and still Mr. Munro had let her come home! He'd only sent her away long enough so nobody would know about it, but *she* knew. It was scandalous. Disgraceful!

Edith wondered just how forgiving he'd be this time, when the man she was catting around with was his own business partner.

CHAPTER THIRTEEN

AT THE SOFT KNOCK ON Della's bedroom door, Erin
looked up from the journal. "Yes?"

"It's Annie, missus. Mr. Munro told me to fetch
you for breakfast."

Erin noticed the sun was lighting the room, not
just the bedside lamp. She had been reading non-
stop since she'd returned from the guesthouse.
Reading and fuming. The thought of facing J.B.
after some of the entries in Della's diary made
breakfast sound unappetizing, to say the least.

"Annie, tell him I won't be down this morning."

There was silence, then Annie cleared her throat.
"Umm...missus...? He was quite insistent, he was.
It's Mr. Wyndham's last morning here at the mansion, and Mr. Munro told me not to listen to
any...er...excuses."

Erin groaned loudly.

"I'm that sorry, missus."

"No, Annie. It's not you I'm angry with." She
narrowed her gaze down at the particularly incrim-

inating entry she'd just finished. "Tell Mr. Munro I'll be down as soon as I'm dressed."

"Yes'm."

Erin hid the diary between the mattresses of Della's bed, then trudged to the closet for a suitable day dress. Her reflection in the bathroom mirror didn't surprise her. Dark circles beneath her angry eyes betrayed the fact that she'd had too little sleep.

Her rage was on Della's behalf. There was only a third or more of the diary to go, but Erin really didn't need to read any more. What she'd learned so far gave her a very good understanding of Della and why she had become the woman she was. The poor girl's story read like a character study in Psychology 101. It was no wonder she acted the way she had.

Erin splashed cool water on her face. Promiscuity had been the least J.B. should have expected after the way he and that wife of his had treated Della. It was a miracle, in Erin's opinion, that Della hadn't murdered J.B. in his sleep years ago.

Pulling Della's brush through her hair, Erin thought of the passages about Waite. She had winced and grimaced through the entire section. It was the only part of the diary where Erin had become angry with Della. Dysfunctional upbringing or not, Della shouldn't have treated the man Erin loved so cruelly. His childhood hadn't been a walk in the park, either. He didn't deserve the pain Della had inflicted.

But then, it was J.B who was responsible. And he deserved every bit of grief Della had given him later in her life. In spades.

"AH, HERE SHE IS, gentlemen," J.B. announced from his place at the head of the table. They all stood. "And looking fresh as the morning dew, as usual."

Oh, I pass inspection, do I? Erin thought irritably, gritting her teeth as a servant pulled out her chair. Where were the compliments when Della needed them? When she'd been a little girl, orphaned and new to your fancy world and scared to death she wouldn't please you. *Where were your flowery words then?*

I wonder, Diary, will I always look like this? I do so hope to outgrow my appearance. Virginia says J.B. complains often to her about my horrid red hair and freckles. I don't want to disappoint him always. I even thought at first that he might someday let me call him "Papa." But what man would want me for a daughter?

Erin sat down at the table next to J.B. and attempted to freeze him with a look. *Fresh as the dew— Pu-leez!*

"Actually, I look like hell, J.B.," she said, then took a long drink of her orange juice. "Oh, but where are my manners? Thank you, dear, and don't you look handsome as always."

Her sarcasm was met with silence, then uncomfortable looks from J.B., Wyndham and Waite, who raised a brow at her.

Wyndham cleared his throat. "Well, you don't look, uh, bad to me, Mrs. Munro. I was telling J.B. just moments ago what a fine representative of Oklahoma womanhood you'll make for the businessmen's wives who'll soon be settling in your state."

"Oh, is that so?"

"Yes, Della. Harrison has decided to tell his clients that Oklahoma, Munro in particular, would be an ideal location for expanding their businesses." J.B. gave her a stern shape-up-your-act look. "I foresee garden parties and bridge games for the wives, Harrison. Della plays a mean game of auction bridge, don't you, dear?"

Diary, you're my only confidante. I'm a terrible girl, a complete failure in my wonderful guardian's eyes. Truly, everyone in his town adores him, and so do I. But I have no social graces. No matter how hard I try to live up to the Munro name, I am an embarrassment to the Munros. I overheard J.B. telling Virginia that I'll never make a good hostess...unless the party is held on horseback. It is truly sad that after two whole years with the Munros, I have managed to improve only my riding skills.

"Auction bridge? No, I detest it, J.B." Erin didn't know what the hell it was, but she couldn't let the opportunity to avenge Della in some small way pass her by. "Do the wives ride horses, Mr. Wyndham? I'm good at that."

Waite's brows almost disappeared under a shock of hair this time. J.B. seemed ready to breathe fire. Wyndham merely shrugged and smiled, apparently not noticing her efforts to annoy the hell out of J.B. "Well, I'm certain some of them do, but those who don't will probably be happy to be instructed by you."

J.B. seemed to relax a bit. Still, he eyed Erin over the rim of his cup, sending heated warnings in her direction.

For all the times he'd made a little girl's heart bleed, for all the harsh words that had torn apart her confidence, for his ironfisted, dictatorial control over the young Della, Erin shot a quelling look right back at him. *Go ahead,* she thought, *mess with me some more. I'm just furious enough, just punchy enough, to screw up this business deal for you, but good.*

J.B. cleared his throat, turning his attention back to Wyndham in the nick of time. "Oh, yes, my Della is an expert horsewoman. She taught Waite how to ride Thoroughbreds, didn't you, darling?"

"Y-yes," Erin answered, her gaze connecting with Waite's for a long moment. She would have given much to know what was going on in his mind at the moment. He was careful not to let any emotion register on his face, but Erin guessed he was thinking of those riding lessons. J.B. had suggested them, and in the course of her instruction, Waite had fallen in love.

Della had been seventeen at the time, and J.B.'s first wife had been dead for a year. It was apparent from what Erin had learned from Della's diary that the girl was so filled with self-loathing by that time that she was incapable of loving anyone. There were some who turned hatred inward, but Della had been the opposite. She became a veritable hellion. Yet, in her heart of hearts, beneath all the scars J.B. and Virginia had inflicted, she had yearned for J.B.'s attention and approval.

When it finally sank in that his approval would never be won, she still fought for his attention. And Waite was her weapon. She had known J.B. would be incensed when he discovered she had been sleeping with Waite, his "fair-haired" boy.

It finally happened as I've told you it would, Diary. J.B. found out. You never believed he would, did you? You probably even thought that if he did, he would ignore it, as he has all my other "escapades." Not this time! God, how I'd hoped my plan would work. And it did. I've loved him forever, Diary. I wanted him to love me, too. Virginia is gone now, and J.B. needs a wife by his side. I'll be that wife. Now that I finally have him...you'll see. I'll change. I'll be just what he needs, everything he wants. Waite MacKinnon was the son he never had—I heard him say it. And I knew if I threatened to run away with Waite, J.B. would do anything to stop me. Even this.

"Ah, look at the time," Wyndham said, clicking shut a pocket watch and rising from his chair. "If you'll be so kind as to lend me your driver, J.B., I'll be on my way to the station."

J.B. blotted at his mouth with his napkin and rose, too. "I'll drive you myself, Harrison. There's the matter of my upcoming trip to Boston. We can discuss it on the way."

"Fine, then. If you can have one of your people bring down my bags...

"Mrs. Munro," he said, smiling widely, "it has been a delightful trip. Most enjoyable. Thank you for having me in your home."

Erin nodded, his graciousness softening her hostility and coaxing a smile to her lips. "It . . . was a pleasure, Mr. Wyndham."

Wyndham left the room, and J.B. made to follow. He turned back in the doorway. "When I get back, you and I are going to have a little talk, Della."

Oh, great. She'd probably pushed him too far. But in a way, she just didn't care anymore.

She watched Waite wipe his mouth with his napkin, then place it carefully beside his plate. He glanced up at Erin, holding up a palm when she opened her mouth to speak.

They heard the sound of the front door closing, and each began to speak.

"We have to talk—"

"I need to talk—"

Erin smiled at him, and at the pleasurable feeling of simply being alone in the room with him. Suddenly her weariness fled . . . and her anger. Oh, how she wished for the one thing she knew she couldn't have—a future with him. Days and months and years of sitting across from him at a breakfast table. "Yes, we need to talk," she said. "But not here. In the guesthouse. You go now. I'll be there in a few minutes. I have something to show you.''

FRANKLIN THOMAS WATCHED from across the boulevard as the Packard left through the main gates of the estate. J. B. Munro, he thought, recognizing the driver. Lord of the manor and all he surveyed. A red mist of fury clouded his vision as he watched the man drive away in his expensive automobile.

It was said Munro could buy and pay for any man in the state, and Franklin had learned from his father not long ago how true that was. His own family had been among the tycoon's victims, hadn't they? Franklin had thought the move to Kansas had been his father's decision, but he'd found out he was wrong. J.B. Munro had wanted the Thomases out of the state. Out of sight, out of mind, out of his town.

Had Franklin's act been one of pure revenge, he would have killed J.B. as well as his wife. But now, apparently, the bitch was alive, after all, and he still wanted justice. Not revenge; simply justice.

He turned his gaze to the mansion, angry that he hadn't finished the job. He calculated ways to gain entrance this time. He had bluffed his way into the house the night of the party by mingling with a large group of latecomers. The servant at the door

had been none the wiser. And it hadn't been difficult enticing Della away. All he'd had to do was
mention Henry and the child.

But now she knew what he looked like. A direct
approach wouldn't work this time.

So he would wait. And watch. Della Munro
would leave the mansion sooner or later. When she
did, Franklin would be ready. This time, there
would be no mistakes.

"WHAT IN GOD'S NAME were you doing at breakfast?"

Erin closed the door behind her, then stepped
over the books that still lay on the floor, making her
way to the sofa where Waite sat staring stonily at
her.

"Well, good morning to you, too," she said with
a smile, setting the diary on the table next to him.

"It's not. A good morning, that is."

She leaned close, brushing her lips lightly across
his frowning mouth, and waited for him to deepen
the kiss. She nearly died of frustration before he
finally tilted his head and caught her mouth with
his, clasping her hands and pulling her down next
to him.

"How can you remain so calm?" he asked,
worry evident in the two lines that formed a vee at

the bridge of his nose. "How can you smile so easily when you know what we've done?"

She shook her head. "We haven't done anything wrong, Waite. I wish I could convince you of that. Besides, I've become very good at acting in the past few days. I'm not calm, it just looks like I am."

Waite gave her a dry look. "If you were aiming for a cool facade at breakfast, I have to say, Della, you're no Mary Pickford."

Erin's lips twitched. "Or Meryl Streep, for that matter," she added. "An actress in the nineties," she explained when he shot her a questioning look. "And I wasn't acting, then. I was furious at J.B. because I found this." She reached across him to get the journal. "I found it on the floor last night before I left. Della must have stuck it behind other books on the shelf. Here . . . read the first page."

He eyed her quizzically for a moment, then took the journal, reading as she requested.

"Your diary?" he asked, looking up from the page.

Erin sighed. "*Her* diary, Waite. And it documents her life from the time she first arrived here as Virginia and J.B.'s ward."

"And . . . ?"

"And that's why I was so . . . so angry. The way she was treated by them, and him especially . . . It's all in there! The emotional abuse, the dysfunctional behavior... She couldn't have been expected to turn out any way other than she did and—What? Why are you frowning again?"

He heaved a loud sigh. "Dysfunctional? Emotional abuse? I know the words but I'm not sure I understand."

"Oh. They're nineties terms. Let's see.... You would probably refer to it as 'extremely strict,' or 'mistreatment.' They've discovered a few things about human behavior since Sigmund Freud's time, Waite. And one of the biggest discoveries is that you can't abuse a child emotionally, treat them as if they have no worth, and then expect them to become stable, happy, functioning adults."

"Abuse? J.B. and Virginia took her—"

Erin lifted a brow at his slip.

Waite rolled his eyes. "I mean, *you.* They took you in when your parents were killed. You were given everything you needed...wanted. A home, those beautiful Thoroughbred horses you love so much, expensive clothes to wear—"

"Love?" Erin prompted, then answered her own question. "They didn't come close to giving her what she really needed. And she was desperate for it. It wasn't her fault that she was left an orphan, but they treated her as though she was an albatross around their necks. They tried to mold her into something she wasn't, then blamed her for their dissatisfaction."

"Sounds as though no one from your time takes responsibility for their actions if nothing they do is their own fault."

Erin gave a wry grin. "Actually, you're not too far off base with that one. A better balance probably could be struck on the whole fault-blame thing."

She suddenly realized exactly what he'd said. "Hey! You just said, 'No one from your time.' Does that mean you're coming around?"

Waite allowed a glimmer of a smile in return. "Let's just say you make it seem possible. The more I listen to you, the easier it is to believe that you aren't from anywhere around here. But still, when I look at you, I see a woman I've known for years. You just have to understand how difficult—"

She brought one of his hands to her lips, bestowing a kiss on his knuckles. It was a start, she thought. Even if, in the end, he was never able to fully believe her incredible story, it felt wonderful to know that he didn't always think of her as Della. "I do. Really, you're talking to someone who can hardly believe it herself."

He nodded. "This diary. Why is it so important to you that I see it?"

"Well, I haven't read all of it yet, but I'm hoping it will give me a clue as to who murdered her. I have a feeling that's why I'm here. I mean, there has to be some reason, right? And I remembered something J.B. said...that someday I'd know why he was so grateful. Until I found this diary, I didn't stop to think about the why of it all. I was just intent on getting back."

Waite closed his eyes and leaned his head against the back of the sofa. "Now you have me completely confused."

"I'm sorry. I didn't tell you everything last night about how I came to be here, did I?"

"I thought you said something about the locket and the portrait—not that I don't have trouble with the story, you understand."

"You get an A for effort," she said with a grin. "The thing is, I met J.B. in *my* time. I know," she said when his head whipped around. "Hard to believe, but J.B. Munro will live to the ripe old age of one hundred and seven. Anyway, my unit—you'll remember I told you about my being a paramedic—was called to the mansion when he suffered a heart attack." Waite swallowed and glanced away. Erin squeezed his hand.

"I'm . . . sorry. I know this must be difficult."

"Go ahead," he murmured, his voice gruff.

"He . . . he knew me. That is, at first he thought I was Della, and kept asking me to forgive him. I thought he was disoriented because of the pain and his advanced age. Then he said, no, I wasn't her, and told me he knew who I was. I was the other one. Erin."

Waite watched her but said nothing.

"It was really eerie, you know? We got him to the hospital, but he . . . died that night. But before he did, he told the night nurse to tell me that someday I would know how grateful he was to me."

"Again, none of this makes sense to me, but gratitude for coming to his aid doesn't seem so odd to me."

"Well, it did to me at first, especially because he knew my name. But I finally wrote it off to coincidence—not the gratitude, but the name business. Anyway, months later, this mansion was opened for tours."

"Tours?"

"Yes. I guess J.B. left the estate to the city, since he died with no heirs. The tour guide told us about Della's murder, Waite. And guess who one of the prime suspects was?"

He sighed, looking more uncomfortable by the moment. "I couldn't imagine."

"You."

"Me!" He jumped to his feet. "I didn't murder her! Why would anybody think— Oh, Lord, what am I saying?"

"I know, I know…. You just can't believe it happened, because if I'm Della, then there was no murder. But there was. It happened, okay? Just stay with me, here," she said wearily. "Anyway, the reason you were one of the suspects was there were rumors that you and Della were having an affair around that time."

"Imagine Della and I having an affair," he muttered dryly.

"Smart-ass," she muttered back. "You disappeared after they found her body. And you were never heard from again."

Waite's jaw worked, and he shoved his hands into his pockets. Turning away from her, he paced to the window that looked out over his friend's estate.

His body language revealed it all. Erin could only see him from behind, but she noted the tension in his shoulders, the hands that were now balled into fists at his sides. He swung around to face her, and the pain in his eyes made Erin wish she'd never told him about the future. But she'd had to. He had to be in on this if she was going to accomplish what now seemed to be her mission here.

She thought of her parents' lecture on that fateful day "back" in the nineties. Only days ago, she mused, but it felt as though she'd lived two lifetimes since then. They'd wanted her to "get a life." Well, she'd gotten one, all right. Never mind that it was someone else's.

She rose from the sofa slowly, an ache in her throat as she approached the man she had fallen in love with. The realization that she didn't have a lifetime to spend with him ripped her apart.

"Waite," she murmured, placing her palm on his jaw. "I didn't tell you all this to hurt you. Oh, I know what you're thinking. How can it hurt when it's all a huge, complicated delusion, a product of Della's overactive imagination, right?"

He tried to look away, but Erin wouldn't allow it. She raised her other hand to his face and forced him to look at her. "But it's not a delusion. Deep inside, you know that."

"I *want* to know it. Want to believe ..."

She nodded. "Finding the diary made me understand why all this has happened. It's not just for Della's sake. *You're* why I'm here."

CHAPTER FOURTEEN

WAITE DIDN'T KNOW whether to keep listening, leave while some of his sanity was still intact or tell *her* to go. But in the end, he continued staring into her eyes, which were the only physical evidence he had that she could be telling the truth. They were darker than before; that hadn't changed.

God, how he wanted to believe! But how could he? Now she was saying her little "journey through time"—he cringed even hearing the words in his mind—was somehow connected with him.

"Me? I'm why you're here?"

"Yes. It makes sense if you'll just use logic."

"Sense! Logic?"

"Okay, okay," she said. "Those might not have been the best words I could have used, but you're in this far, so you might as well listen to the rest of my lunacy, right?"

Waite's lips twitched. Who knew? Maybe she *wasn't* Della. Della Munro had never shown him a humorous side. She'd never joked or teased, and had thought him irritating when he'd tried to coax a smile out of her. He liked the smile that curved this woman's lips and sparked in her eyes right now. Her *darker* green eyes, he told himself again.

"Right," he said, and gave in to a smile, too.

"Oh, that's a killer," she said, her voice breathy. She reached to trace his bottom lip with her thumb. "You don't do that very often, do you?"

No, he supposed he didn't. He hadn't given it much thought, but what had there been to smile about in the past several years? Making more and more money? Enlarging the Munro empire? "No, I don't."

"I'm going to take it as a compliment. In fact, I think I'll take credit."

He covered her hand with his and pressed a kiss on her fingertips. "You should." It didn't matter if this woman who called herself Erin was in reality Della, she was a changed Della. And he loved the changes. Loved *her*. It might be insane, but hell, he was close to deciding that insanity might not be such a bad thing, after all.

She caught her breath.

"What? Is something wrong?"

"No, I just—" She gently wrested her hands from his, her eyes wide as she backed a step away. "Tell me if I'm deluded about that look. Does it mean… I mean, could it possibly be because you… Because if it is … I—I just—"

"You just what?" He was smiling again. At the blush in her cheeks, the way she couldn't finish a sentence . . . and just because it felt good to smile again.

"I just . . . I love you, too."

He pulled her into his arms, held her as close as was humanly possible. Hell . . . wasn't that where his soul would be consigned for the sin he'd so willingly committed? He had never been religious but had always respected the laws of God and man. Until now, it seemed. Because holding her next to his heart, tight in his embrace, he didn't give a damn where he might end up. "That's what it meant," he said, and kissed her. She was crying. "What's this?"

"Oh, it's awful," she said, sobbing quietly. She wiped at the tears with the backs of her hands. "I mean it's wonderful, but it's awful, too. I . . . I wanted to find someone like you, and I needed a new life . . . and poof, here you are, and here's a life—boy, what a life!—only it's someone else's, and I can't keep it *or* you. I know I'll have to go back just as surely as I know what it is I'm here to do, and—" she sniffled, looked up into his eyes, then sobbed again "—and it's just not fair. I know that sounds childish, but damn it, you'd think after all I've been through . . ."

Waite could do no more than shake his head and stroke her cheek with his thumb. All this talk of having someone else's life and going back and forth through time . . . Well . . . what could he say to her? It was just so damned crazy. Wasn't it?

He felt a twinge of panic. What if it was all true? He didn't want to lose her, either.

"You don't have to give me up. I don't want that to happen, either." He leaned forward, placing a whisper-soft kiss on the tip of her nose. "I want to tell J.B. about us."

She pulled back, her eyes suddenly wide with alarm. "No! Are you crazy? You can't tell J.B.!"

"Yes, I can. And I will." Guilt made his chest feel tight. "He doesn't deserve what I've done to him. But more than that, he doesn't deserve insult on top of injury—to be lied to about it. No one does.

"Stop shaking your head and listen to me," he ordered, anchoring her face with his hands. "I think he'll give you a divorce. Your version of history will come true then, won't it? Because I want us to leave here. We won't have to be apart."

She squeezed her eyes shut. "No, no, no. Waite, I've told you, I'm not his to divorce. And you haven't done anything to him!"

When she opened her eyes, Waite saw that her sorrow had been replaced with anger. She folded her arms beneath her breasts. "And it's not *my* version of history, it's what really happens! I've been trying to tell you that!

"I put it all together after finding the diary. Della didn't just write about you, J.B. and Virginia. There are a bunch of references to other of her acquaintances . . . friends, enemies. I haven't finished reading yet because I was summoned to breakfast by his royal highness, but when I do, I think I'll get some clues as to who killed her. I'll clear your name and you won't have to leave."

"You think you're here to find a killer?"

"What other reason could there be? This was someone's grand design," she said, her expression still piqued, "not an accident. There are simply too many coincidences."

"Coincidences?"

"Like the fact that I look just like her, yet we're not related. And what about the locket? You gave it to her, and it was your mother's, right?"

"Yes."

"Yet in 1994, I end up with it. I was born forty-one years after her death, yet I end up with a locket that's connected to you. I also met J.B. Munro on the last day of his life and he told a nurse I'll know someday why he's so grateful to me."

"Again, I think he was merely appreciative for—"

"Nope. I don't buy it. After reading Della's diary and finding out just what you have always meant to J.B.—the son he never had—I think that he was grateful to me because I found the real murderer. I saw him, the man with the beard. I'm the only one who can identify him, Waite. And that would clear your name."

He raked a hand through his hair. "Della—"

"Erin," she insisted.

He decided to go along with her. "Erin."

Her smile was beautiful, lighting up her entire face and making her eyes sparkle. "Do you know how much I've wanted to hear you say it, Waite?"

"I . . . yes, I think I do, but—" He turned away from her, looking outside again. He knew how much she wouldn't want to hear what he said next. "I will still leave, Erin. No matter what it is that you're here to do. Leaving has been on my mind more and more lately, and now I know it's what I have to do. Come with me."

EDITH COULDN'T GAUGE Mr. Munro's expression. He didn't seem furious at that slut of a wife, as she had hoped. And he wasn't grief stricken, either. He didn't seem . . . anything at all. Aside from the tic beneath his eye, his expression was flat, revealing nothing.

She wondered what that meant. Maybe he didn't believe what she'd told him and was about to fire her on the spot. She wrung her hands. For all that she complained about the sinful goings-on in this mansion, J. B. Munro paid his servants better than any of the other wealthy men in town.

He rubbed at the tic, his cold blue eyes still expressionless, and reached into the top drawer of his desk. Edith swallowed. "Mr. Munro, I hope you won't think of lettin' me go for what I told you. I—"

He cut her off with a sharp glance from those cold, blue eyes, and pulled out a leather-bound book. Flipping it open, he bent to write something on the first page. A bank draft? she wondered. From what some of the other servants had told her, Munro was forever and always paying off someone to keep their mouth closed about some scandal or other.

Good thing his pockets were so deep, she reflected. They'd have to be with that wife, wouldn't they? Her attitude brightened considerably at the thought that she might reap some rewards out of this. "I'm good at keeping my mouth shut, sir. You can count on that."

"Can I?"

"Oh, yes, sir. I know how to button my lip but good." Edith craned her neck, hoping to get an idea of just how much he wanted it buttoned. Her eyes widened when she saw the amount. A fortune! He was giving Edith a fortune to make sure she kept quiet! She could hardly believe her good luck. Her breathing quickened.

"That's good." He slid the draft across his desk. "I expect you to be packed and gone within the hour. Out of my home . . . out of Munro."

Edith's mouth gaped. "You . . . want me to leave town? But . . . I don't have no people anywhere else. Or no friends. Been here since I was a kid. I don't have no other home besides this one."

Munro rose from his chair, circling to the front of the desk. "With what I just paid you, you can buy new friends wherever you go."

"But, I—"

"An hour, Edith. Unless, of course, you don't want the money."

"No! No, I . . . guess I'll be leaving," she said quietly, then snatched up the draft.

"Good. We have an understanding, then. That money pays for your silence. But just in case you decide you can't keep that lip buttoned, I want you away from my town."

"HE'LL SEE YOU NOW, Mr. MacKinnon," Simmons said, holding open J.B.'s office door. The dour butler seemed in high spirits for once, whistling as he disappeared down the hallway, carrying a tray that Waite assumed held the remains of J.B.'s lunch.

Taking a deep breath, Waite stepped to the door, his gut twisted in knots. There had been a time in his younger days when confrontations about anything with J.B. had filled him with apprehension. Now it was only the fierce nagging guilt he'd felt since last night that ate away at him. He had to tell him, and now was the time—no matter what Della thought.

J.B. looked up from the paperwork on his desk, freezing him in his tracks with the look of quiet fury in his eyes. Waite had prepared himself for J.B.'s anger—felt he deserved it, of course—but he'd expected to see it *after* he told J.B., not *before*. Damn! He hadn't wanted J.B. to hear of it from anyone else. "You already know, don't you?"

"I was told by a servant who saw Della leave the guesthouse so late last night." His anger seemed to deflate slightly, and pain shaded his eyes. "I had thought maybe you had an explanation. *Hoped,* I guess, is the better word. When you asked to see me, I held on to the chance that you'd tell me nothing untoward—"

"Don't, J.B." Waite suffered along with his friend. He'd been Waite's only family, the only family he'd had since he was a boy. To think that he'd repaid him with this...

"It did happen. I won't lie to you. And you can't know how deeply I regret the pain I've caused you."

"Regret? You deeply *regret?*" J.B.s laugh was harsh and bitter. "That seems a weak word under the circumstances, wouldn't you say?"

Waite didn't answer. He deserved everything the older man had to say.

J.B. pounded the top of his desk with his fist, giving full vent to his anger. "You were at the top of your class in college, Waite!" he shouted. "Surely a man with your intelligence shouldn't find trouble communicating his thoughts. God, and after all I've done for you!"

Waite didn't comment. J.B. had given him his first break, but Waite had worked his ass off for everything else. Nothing had been given him, save that first job. "I'm grateful for all you've done for me, J.B. That hasn't changed."

"Grateful," he spat. "This is the way you show your gratitude? After all I've invested in you, taught you, you show me your deepest apprecia-tion with disloyalty? This is the repayment I'm supposed to be happy with after taking you into my company, my home...my family. God, how could you do it, Waite? How? Do you hate me so much for marrying her? Is this your revenge for—"

"No," Waite cut him off quickly. "It wasn't revenge. I got over you marrying her a long time ago, J.B."

"I don't believe you."

"You have every reason not to. But it's the truth."

"If it is, then explain to me why you did something this stupid! Damn it, Waite, I thought you had more sense than this. You've never been a man to forsake your integrity and your morals for the likes of someone so far beneath you. A slut like Della."

Three days ago, J.B.'s words wouldn't have sparked this outrage in Waite. Now they suffused him with rage. "She's your wife, man! A member of your family since she was a child! How can you say that about her?"

A look of surprise showed in J.B.'s eyes. "Because it's true, of course. I have trouble believing that you, of all men, would forget that."

J.B. pointed a finger at him. "You could have been ruined by her when you were young, Waite, but I didn't allow it. Do you realize the sacrifice I made to make sure your future wasn't put at risk for that worthless piece of trash?"

Worthless. Trash. Waite ground his teeth. "Shut up, J.B! Don't say another damn word!" It took a supreme effort of will to keep from pounding J.B. with his fists. Eri—no, Della's words came back to him. Waite hadn't thought of J.B.'s treatment of her as harmful, he had only seen him as a strict disciplinarian. Now he realized the man hated Della. "You despise her, don't you?"

J.B. lifted a brow. "Has she ever given me reason not to?"

"She was your daughter, J.B!"

"She was my ward, not my blood. And trouble from the moment Virginia and I took her in." He sighed. "I needed a wife, Waite, and I needed to save you from being destroyed. It was a mistake not sending her away after this last ordeal. I see that now, of course. And I'll correct my mistake."

Waite remembered her saying she feared J.B. would send her to an asylum. Dear Lord, she hadn't been exaggerating. "No, J.B., you won't send her away. She'll be leaving of her own accord. She should have done it years ago, in fact. With me. But I, too, can correct my mistakes."

J.B.'s astonishment was complete. His jaw hung slack and he shook his head slowly. "You've lost your mind, haven't you?"

"Give her a divorce, J.B. Think of *her* for once in your life. God knows, had you ever treated her with even the smallest measure of kindness, things might have turned out differently."

J.B.'s jaw clenched. "I am willing to forgive you your momentary lapse in sanity—forgive you, send Della where she won't cause more trouble and get on with our lives. Don't be a fool, Waite. If you have a brain in your head, use it! She will destroy you."

Waite was stunned. Not at J.B.'s last comment; he'd heard that from the man before. It was his total lack of compassion for Della that was so astonishing. Waite knew their marriage had been a sham, and he'd witnessed J.B.'s anger at her whenever she had "misbehaved," but he hadn't imagined J.B. didn't care for her at all...hadn't imagined he held her in such contempt.

"Don't do this, Waite. You'll lose everything. I promise you that."

Waite felt hollow inside. Where once he'd admired his mentor, had respected him and prized their friendship, he now could only feel pity for the man. It pained him to discover he'd been so wrong, so blind about J.B.

"I pictured this scenario quite differently, J.B.," he said in a low voice. "You say you'll forgive me. I would have thought your pride would forbid such a thing."

"Foolish to be prideful, Waite. Don't get me wrong, I am angry with you. Disappointed. But we can make a new start."

"Disappointed..." Waite's mouth tightened in a grim line. "But not because she's your wife. I slept with her, this woman you're married to, and all you feel is...disappointed. Not because vows have been broken, or even because you're sick at heart over our betrayal, but because, like a disobedient child, I went against your plans for me."

J.B. looked at him with exasperation. "You didn't think I would be disappointed? Waite, there might only be ten years' difference in our ages, but you've been like a son to me, not just a business associate. When I see you take a wrong path, of course it disappoints me." He rose and came around the desk to him, his eyes softening as he placed a hand on Waite's shoulder. "It's what fathers do, Waite. They want only the best for their sons."

Disgusted, Waite shoved J.B.'s hand away. "And what is it they want for their daughters, you bastard?" He turned on his heel and strode toward the door, turning back to look at him one last time. "She's not worthless trash. She was only made to feel that way by you. You can give her the divorce or not. One way or the other, she's coming with me."

"Don't do this, Waite," J.B. pleaded, striding forward. "She'll ruin you and you know it!"

"No. It appears she's saved me."

I love him, Diary. That shocks you, I am sure. Or maybe it doesn't. Maybe you knew all along that there is a heart, a small capacity to love buried somewhere deep within me. Certainly there has to be, for how could I feel this way without it!

I thought he was a silly boy at first, though handsome. I met him at the golf course where he was caddying for the summer.

He didn't know who I was!—I found out later that his family was new to Munro. I considered his flirting with me quite amusing at first. Good Lord, he wore Oxford bags, so I knew he was college age and probably as green as grass. Nothing more irritating than a clumsy boy who thinks petting in the back seat of his father's Maxwell is just the thing! But I was particularly irritated at J.B. that day for some reason I've forgotten now, so you know what I did next, Diary.

Yes, I told him to meet me later in the woods at the edge of the Munro property. Can you believe it? He referred to it as a date! And he wanted to pick me up at my front door! I told him my father was strict and didn't allow "dates."

Diary, he treated me as no other man I've ever known! And, as you are aware, I've known too many to count. We talked. Amazingly enough, it was all he wanted to do! I didn't know what to say at first. Me, shy! I never just talk to men. So I asked him about himself. And I found out that he is older than he looks. Though younger than me, it is only by two years. I also discovered that he is very religious. It made me quite uneasy, and I think you know why. I kept expecting lightning to strike the poor man just because of who he was with.

I feel guilty about meeting him. And about not telling him who I really am. It's been three weeks since that first time, and he deserves my honesty. If anyone deserves it, he does. But, Diary, I will lose him if I tell, so I have made sure no one has seen us together and sworn him to secrecy. He told me last night that he loves me and wants to be with me forever. He also told me of his plans to become a minister. That's right . . . Della and a minister. It would be hilarious if it weren't so heartbreaking.

He kissed me last night. For the first time. And he told me I am beautiful.

ERIN TRIED TO SWALLOW past the tears that had gathered in her throat. *Oh, Della,* she thought, closing the diary, *I'm so glad you had him, at least. There was so much sorrow for you, and you needed some happiness.*

She glanced around the bedroom Della had slept in, wondering if she'd written these entries while sitting in the chair where Erin sat now. Had she lain in that bed and fantasized about a life with the man who thought she was beautiful? Did she ever gaze into the gilt-framed mirror on the wall and see past her own image of herself to the beauty he saw? Perhaps not, for she had hidden the diary in the guesthouse. Or had that been later?

Erin wanted to know more, but then again, she didn't. She was curious, of course. And she still had found no clues as to who might have murdered Della. So it was imperative that she read on. But in a way she wished that the diary had ended with those words.

And he told me I am beautiful.

Erin opened the book at the page where she had left off and read on. Through five more entries, Della told of their romance. They continued to keep their meetings a secret, though her love had wanted to meet her family and make his intentions known. Della was consumed with guilt for deceiving him, but she was desperately in love. She told her diary that she knew how selfish it was, but the thought of losing the only love she'd ever known was devastating.

Erin's apprehension grew with each word she read. As though she were living the scenes right along with Della, her heart soared when she wrote of the man telling her for the first time that he loved her. Her palms sweated at Della's terror that J.B. had become suspicious.

She gasped aloud when Della disclosed she had become pregnant with her lover's child.

CHAPTER FIFTEEN

PREGNANT!

Erin's heart rate faltered, her gaze racing back to the date at the top of the entry she had just read. Could that have been—

Yes! It had happened four years ago. Dear God, this was it, Erin realized—the scandal that had caused Della's banishment from the mansion! This was what Edith had tried to tell Annie about before J.B. had interrupted them that first morning!

Erin swiftly read on.

Della had been overjoyed to discover she carried her lover's child, but she was frightened, too. This would destroy everything. She couldn't tell her lover, wouldn't allow this to wreck his chances for a future in the ministry; his good name would be ruined forever. And if J.B. found out, she was certain her fate would not be a pretty one. Marriage to J.B. hadn't turned out as Della had hoped. They'd been estranged from each other in every way that counted almost from the very beginning.

As Erin read on, the story of Della's emotional ordeal unfolded. She tried ending the affair, but her love wouldn't have it. He refused to believe her when she told him she didn't love him anymore, and he threatened to go to J.B., whom he still thought was Della's father. He was going to ask for her hand in marriage. Finally, realizing the only way to drive her lover away would be to tell him the truth, the complete truth, Della began by spilling the news about the baby.

It didn't affect him as she'd hoped. He was thrilled, filled with wonder that they had created a child. Della was stunned, speechless and in tears when he had grinned like a complete idiot, then grabbed her up and twirled her in circles.

Erin smiled. What a guy. For a man in the 1920s, and one who was going to become a minister, no less, he must have loved her very much indeed. But she dreaded reading what would come next, how he would react to the whole truth.

He didn't take the rest of her news well. He became angry, in fact, just as Della had known he would. The misery in his eyes had nearly killed her, but she watched him leave their meeting place that day with a small portion of relief in her heart. It was over now. She would grieve for her lost love the rest of her life, but she was thankful she had saved him from further shame and humiliation. She had saved him from herself.

Tears stung Erin's eyes. She fought to hold them back, desperate to know what happened to Della and the baby. She knew from Edith's gossip that Della had been sent away, but what had happened after that? Did she have the baby? Lose it? If it had been born, where was it now?

Erin forged ahead.

Della hadn't thought she'd needed to save the man from himself as well as her. She'd had no idea that he would be foolhardy enough to come to J.B. and demand that he give her a divorce so they could marry. J.B. had been enraged, more so than Della had ever seen him. He had threatened her lover with everything he could think of, including the financial ruin of his family. He wouldn't allow scandal to touch the Munro household. On this, he was immovable. And the young man was just as undaunted, determined to have Della and his child with him, where they belonged.

But Della had known what J.B. was capable of. She knew there was no possible way any man could win when pitted against him. So when he lied, telling her young man that he and Della had been sleeping together, too, Della went along with it. She had shrugged as if the whole matter meant less to her than a tear in one of her expensive gowns, and said that either man could be the father. Watching her love's spirit die before her very eyes, she died inside, too, but twisted the knife with the words: "What does it matter who the father is, as long as I continue to live in the manner I've become accustomed to? And you could never give me that."

She never saw him again. He'd left, of course, and his family had accepted J.B.'s generous offer to "relocate." Before being quietly sent to an unwed mothers' home in Missouri, Della had pleaded with J.B. to let her have the baby and raise it as theirs. But he wouldn't allow it. He'd set plans in motion for the child to be placed in an orphanage near the home she'd stayed in to have the baby. This was her next entry.

Dear Diary, I have given birth to a son. He is quite beautiful, though I had hoped he would have his father's dark hair instead of my own horrid red. He does have his father's name. I insisted upon it. Henry.

There were several more entries. Some spoke of Della's leaving the child at the orphanage, some of her return to the mansion. She'd been almost suicidal the day she had tenderly kissed her child goodbye, mourning her loss as profoundly as she'd loved the man who had given him to her.

And she had come home forever changed. J.B. had taken the two people she loved most in the world away from her, and she had never again thought of him as the god of her youth.

She also never truly gave up her ties to the child. Unbeknownst to J.B., she found ways to continue visiting the child at the orphanage. She funneled every bit of money she could put her hands on into the organization, on one condition: that the child not be adopted out.

Erin closed the book, her hands trembling and her mind reeling. The last entry Della had made in the diary had been only six months ago, which meant the child was very likely still living in the orphanage Della had named.

And the child's name was Henry. Dear God, *Henry*.

Erin's father's name. And Della's son had the same birthday.

ERIN RAN THE ENTIRE WAY to the guesthouse. She nearly knocked Annie over in the hallway again, putting her off when the maid informed her J.B. wanted to see her in his office. Now her sides ached and her lungs burned from the cold, but she didn't slow down, not until she reached the guesthouse porch. She wrenched open the door, then nearly collided with Waite, who was holding a suitcase in his hands.

"Waite, you have to take me—" she fought to catch her breath "—to Missouri."

He set down his suitcase, a cautious smile in his eyes. "You've changed your mind? You want to leave with me now?"

She frowned at the suitcase, still breathing fast and hard. "No...I mean, I do want you to take me to Missouri, but it's only temporary. You're talking permanently, aren't you? I thought you were going to mull this over for a few days."

"That is what I told you, but—"

"Damn it, Waite! You didn't tell him, did you?"

"I did."

She groaned. "Oh, no. What have you done!"

"What I've done is something that should have been done long ago. Besides, one of the servants who saw you leaving here last night got to him before I did. He already knew."

She blinked in surprise. "Saw me—"

"Yes, and went straight to J.B., it seems."

Waite looked somewhat saddened, but not torn apart over the dissolution of their friendship. "Was he as angry as we expected?" she asked.

"Yes, but only because I won't be fulfilling his plans for my future. You were right. He never gave a damn about you...only about whether you would ruin me." He stroked her cheek with a fingertip. "I told him you had saved me."

"You're a good man, Waite MacKinnon. You came to her defense. And who knows, maybe you're right. Maybe getting the hell away from him will be best for you."

"You're what's best for me. And whether you were going to agree to come with me or not, I was going to get you away from here somehow. Away from him."

Erin felt shrouded in sorrow, and stepped into his arms when he set down the suitcase and opened them to her. She clung tightly, wishing...hoping...yearning. She no longer felt she was living someone else's existence, because she knew now that Della had had the love of her life. So had she. Even knowing it couldn't be, she fantasized that his embrace would be there for her whenever she needed it, throughout time.

A fantasy. That's all it was, all it ever could be. "Waite, I read the rest of her diary." She moved out of his arms. "She...had a child."

"What?"

"Four years ago. Think back, Waite. She was gone for nearly a year. J.B. sent her away to an unwed mothers' home in Missouri to give birth to the baby. A son."

Waite looked incredulous. "A son! J.B. would never send his wife away to have his son. He always wanted—"

"The baby wasn't his."

His eyes widened with shock, then clouded with doubt. Erin held up a palm to forestall anything he had to say. "There's no time to try to convince you again that I'm not her. And no time to discuss this next little tidbit. I think that son is another of the coincidences I was telling you about earlier. He'd be about three years old by now, and still in the orphanage in Missouri. I have to see him. I have to know."

"You want me to take you there."

"Yes."

"And after that?"

"I'm not sure. But if this baby is who I think he is, I'll have to leave."

FRANKLIN'S BLOOD RAN cold when he saw her in the passenger seat of the automobile. The image he had thought he would carry with him forever had been of her lifeless form lying on the cold ground in that cave. Seeing her alive, seeing her talking to the man who sat behind the steering wheel as they drove away from the estate, sent a chill through his body.

He fired up the engine of his own automobile—
the run-down Maxwell he'd purchased upon arriv-
ing back in Munro. Then he set off after them.
Some way, somehow, he would have to separate
Della Munro from her companion.

"OH, MRS. MUNRO!" The woman behind the desk
rose from her chair, a smile on her lips. Her hair
was unfashionably long, but neatly pinned up, and
she wore a plain, serviceable outfit. The nameplate
on her desk read, Mrs. Phillips. It was clear from
the look of respect in her eyes that Della had been
an important patron. She gave Waite a quick, curious look, then centered her gaze back on Erin.
"It's been a long while since we've seen you. And I
have to discuss something of utmost import—"

"I want to see him," Erin interrupted. "He *is*
still here, isn't he?"

"Oh, yes, of course, but—"

"We can discuss whatever it is later, please."
Erin's eagerness to see the child made her words
sound curt and impatient, but she couldn't help
that. Her father. This child could be her own father! She was beside herself with nerves and anticipation. The three-hour drive from Munro to this
Missouri border town had her in a state of extreme
anxiety.

"Of course, Mrs. Munro. I'll bring him immediately." Mrs. Phillips disappeared through a door Erin thought must lead to the children's quarters or dormitories that she and Waite had seen as they'd approached the home.

She glanced at Waite, trying to read his expression. He had been silent for most of the trip, and Erin had wondered what he thought of all this. Was he still close to believing that Della and Erin were two separate people? Or had this last revelation convinced him the injury to her head had sent "Della" over the edge?

At least he was here, and that said something.

"She knew my face, Waite. And she's gone to get the little boy. It really happened as Della wrote it."

One brow lifted as he regarded her. "Did you think I didn't believe you?"

"I don't know what to think." She bit her lip, and began to pace, needing an outlet for her nervous energy. "You were so quiet the whole way here. I guess I could use a clue or two."

"I'm in the same situation. A clue to this puzzle would be nice," he said. "Honestly? I'm very much afraid that all you've told me isn't true. I want you to be Erin. As crazy as your story is, I want it to be real." His voice lowered to a husky whisper. "Because I love Erin. Everything about her. I can see myself with her for the rest of my life."

"I love you, too, but it's not possible—"

The door swung open, and Erin spun around. The woman came back into the room, a carrot-topped boy of about three in her arms.

Erin heard Waite's quick intake of breath. Her own caught in her throat. Oh, Lord, she thought when the child's eyes lighted with happiness upon spotting her. She had known who this boy might be, but all she could think at the moment was, *How? How on earth is this possible?*

He scrambled out of the woman's grasp and ran to Erin, who stooped down in time to catch him in her arms.

"You comed back," he said, wrapping his small arms around her neck. "You always do."

Tears burned behind Erin's eyes. For Della. For this child. For herself. She blinked to keep them back as she held his tiny body tightly, not wanting him to see her tears.

"Yes. I came back," she said, her voice trembling. "Here, let me look at you." She leaned back, smiling into his moss green eyes—so like Della's . . . so like hers. Here was the connection, she thought with awe, taking his sweet face between her palms. Finally she knew why she and Della looked so much alike. Her grandmother. Della was her *grandmother!*

She shook her head in wonder, then chuckled when he imitated her action with a mischievous grin. "Such a comedian." She swiped at his nose with her thumb.

"Who's he?" Henry asked in a stage whisper, pointing in Waite's direction.

Waite stepped forward, and held out his hand. Henry took it with his smaller one and shook it. "My name is Waite," he said, then glanced at Erin with a raised brow.

"This is Henry," she told him in answer to his silent question.

"I'm pleased to meet you, Henry."

The boy grinned from one cute little ear to the other, continuing the handshake with vigor. And Erin's heart turned over in her chest. She loved that adorable smile...had loved it forever. Her thoughts turned to Della again, and she ached anew for the woman's loss. *Damn you to hell, J. B. Munro,* she thought. *Damn you for taking her son from her.*

"That's some handshake, Henry." Waite pulled his hand away and gave a mock wince. "Some grip."

"Yes, sir. I think I'm the strongdest boy here."

Waite chuckled. "I don't doubt it for a minute."

Henry grasped Erin's hand in his. "We gonna play, today? Like always?" he asked her, anticipation shining in his eyes.

"Well...yes. Of course we are. Like always."

"Come on, then. You know how I like them swings."

ERIN HADN'T WANTED IT to end. She could have pushed Henry on the swings, played chase, and dug in the dirt with him for hours more, but the sun had started its descent and Henry's tummy had begun rumbling for his dinner. She thought about asking Waite if they could stay in town and do this again tomorrow, but she knew it was only delaying the inevitable.

Waite held her hand in his as they walked back to the office. She glanced up a time or two, noticing the concern in his eyes. "I'll be all right," she said, her voice husky with tears she refused to shed. She had been given a miracle...the chance to see her own father as a boy. And Henry had gotten to see his "mother" again. A miracle. It was a joyful experience, not an occasion for tears.

When they reentered the reception area, Mrs. Phillips was there to meet them.

"Mrs. Munro, I can't tell you what these visits mean to Henry. He's one of our more well-adjusted children. And I think that's due to you continuing to see him. None of the others' mothers do, you understand."

Not for the first time since suspecting Della's child was her father, Erin wondered about Henry being in the orphanage. Had she known her father was adopted, she might have made the connection between Della and herself from the beginning. But either her father hadn't known it himself or he had kept it secret from the family. "He does seem to be a normal, happy child," she said.

"Yes. He is. But I must ask you to reconsider releasing your rights as his mother, Mrs. Munro. I know how you love him, but this is such an unusual situation. You have been so generous in your patronage of the orphanage, and we appreciate it, as you know. We've kept our promise and made sure that Mr. Munro never got word of your visits. But we have two new couples who are quite taken with little Henry. Both families are wonderful, God-fearing people. I'm sure you'll approve of them. And they so want him for their son, Mrs. Munro. I think it would be in the boy's best interests for you to at least consider letting them adopt him. He needs a family."

Erin stared at the woman, unable to form a single word. This was Della's son, but she was gone now. He was also Erin's father. But surely this wasn't her decision to make. It would eventually happen, of course. Henry became Shirley's brother, Charles and Esther Sawyer's son. But what if neither of these families were the Sawyers? What would she do then?

Waite spoke up. "I need to talk privately with Mrs. Munro if you don't mind."

The woman nodded. "I'll just leave you these files," she said, picking them up off her desk and handing them to Erin. "They're the forms both families filled out."

When she'd left the room, Erin flipped open the first folder. Emma and Seth Johnson. She frowned, closing it.

"Della." Waite took the files from her. "You don't have to do this."

"Waite," she said, impatient, "it's Erin, not Della. And of course I have to—"

"He already has a mother—you. You love him and want him with you. Don't go back to J.B. Take your son and come with me. We can raise him."

Erin closed her eyes. "Oh, Waite...I thought maybe you were coming around. Maybe you finally believed me." She sighed and took his hand, leading him to a divan. They sat, and she gently took the other folder from him. "I want to show you something. Something that might finally make you understand. Don't you know who Henry is? Didn't it occur to you at all?"

"He's your son. Anyone could see that."

"He's not my son, Waite. He's my father." She opened the second folder, praying that the paperwork inside would back her up. It did, and she sighed with relief. There at the top of the page were her grandparents' names, the grandparents she'd always thought were blood relations.

"'Charles and Esther Sawyer,'" he read slowly.

"And no, Waite. I didn't already know about these people, then use their name in my unbelievable story. You heard the woman. She told me all of this as though it were news, not something I was already aware of. It's all true, Waite. Everything I've told you. You wanted to believe it, and you can."

He shook his head. It occurred to her suddenly that she had more proof. She reached into the pocket of her coat—Della's coat—and brought out the driver's license and money she had pulled from her jeans pocket before asking Waite to bring her here. At the time, she had thought only about using the money to get here on her own, had Waite refused her request. She had been too preoccupied with thoughts of her father, the orphanage and Della's tragic past to remember she had evidence of her identity right here in her coat pocket.

"Look at this," she said, placing the license in his hand. "It's a horrible picture, of course. They always are. But it's me." She pointed out her name,

Erin Jane Sawyer, and her year of birth, 1966. "Color photography, Waite. If nothing else will convince you..."

"'Oklahoma, Native America,'" he read from the top of the card. Then he reached for the paper and coins in her hands. Spotting dates on the bills, frowning over a Susan B. Anthony coin, he looked up at her, then down at the names on the adoption form again. A smile dawned in his eyes, then reached his lips. "God, it's true."

"Well, it took you long enough!" she teased, then reached up to place a kiss on his mouth.

He chuckled, handing back her money and license, then captured her face with his hands. His lips moved slowly, warmly over hers, and Erin could taste his joy, his happiness. The guilt had weighed more heavily on him than she had imagined, because the tone and texture of this kiss was like none of the others he'd given her. She could feel his smile through the kiss, and yes, even his relief.

"I love...Erin Sawyer," he said, wonder in his voice and in his eyes as he gazed down at her.

She smiled, knowing this moment would be one she'd remember always. Wherever she ended up, those four words would reside in her heart and mind forever. "And I love Waite MacKinnon." She touched his cheek with her fingertips. "Remember that. No matter what happens."

THEY WERE TRAVELING BACK to Oklahoma, back to the estate most likely, Franklin realized, as he kept a discreet distance behind them in the Maxwell.

He had felt enraged when he'd watched them enter the orphanage. Henry had told him about the child when it was born, but he hadn't known it had been placed in an orphanage. Franklin had discovered that for himself...from Della.

He had never imagined that Della Munro would visit the boy. How could that be when she didn't care about anyone besides herself? His heart pumped black venom when he thought of her still able to see their son while his brother lay cold in his grave.

He had wanted to kill her then and there. But that would have been too risky. Too public. Better that he kill her at the mansion.

WAITE PULLED THE CAR under the portico, waving away the servant who'd stepped out of the mansion, and approached Erin's side of the automobile.

Erin. He took her hand, squeezing it in a gesture of comfort. Her sadness over leaving Henry had slowly lifted with the stories she began telling Waite about her father. The little boy in the orphanage had grown up to be the parent Waite had always longed for—protective, caring, loving.

But a new emotion had claimed her just after they crossed the Oklahoma border. Waite had watched it increase with every mile that brought them closer to Munro. A different type of sadness had come over her. Deeper, more intense. She wouldn't talk to him, and seemed on the verge of crying at any moment.

"Are you worried about telling him about Della?"

She shook her head. "I was at one time. But not now. Now I'm more concerned about punching him out if he reacts the way I think he will. After reading the diary, I know it won't matter to him as much as it should that she's dead."

Waite's jaw clenched. She was probably right. After all he'd learned, J.B. would be relieved to be rid of his wife. "Yes. I understand."

"You're really not angry at her anymore, are you? After what she did to you, you do understand."

He nodded. "I only wish I had known it then. Maybe things would have turned out differently."

"Maybe." Her voice was quiet, her head bowed over their clasped hands. "But then I wouldn't have met you, would I?" She looked up at him. "As selfish as it sounds, I'm almost glad things weren't different. I met you, had this time with you. And I'm sorry if my happiness was at my own grandmother's expense, but . . .

"She had her Henry, and I had you. I'm glad for it."

Waite's gut twisted. He sensed what was coming. "Had. You're telling me goodbye."

She squeezed her eyes shut. One tear escaped and rolled down her cheek. "Yes. I have to go back."

"Because of your father."

"Yes. And because I don't think I have a choice here. I'm no expert at this time-travel business, but I'm not sure nature will allow it. Until I saw Pop, I didn't even stop to realize there's another reason why I can't stay."

He brushed the tear away with his thumb, his heart breaking into tiny pieces. "Why, Erin?"

"Because I'm his daughter. I can't exist here, in his time, when I was actually born forty-one years from now. You understand that, don't you?"

"No," he said wryly. "I don't understand any of it, actually. I only know I want you to stay."

She nodded. "You don't know how much I want that, too."

"I'M GOING TO CHANGE into the clothes I came in," she told Waite as they climbed the stairs to Della's room. "Then you can help me get into the tunnels so I can find the locket. Maybe J.B. will be back by then and I can tell him."

"And maybe he won't." Waite held her hand tightly in his, memorizing the feel of it. There would only be memories, he thought, once she was gone. "You might have to stay longer."

She gave him a sad smile. At the bedroom door, she lifted their joined hands to her mouth, kissing his knuckles before opening the door.

"Oh, missus! You've come back!" Annie rushed forward. "He was so angry when he found out you left. Went wild, he did. I—I couldn't believe what I was seein'. He just acted like a madman! And he tore it up! Took a knife to it. Oh, she's gonna be so mad, I tell him, but he wouldn't listen. By the saints, I've niver seen the likes of—"

"Annie, calm down." Erin took hold of the maid's trembling hands. "Now slow down. Tell me what happened."

"Mr. Munro," she continued, then shot Waite a wary look.

"It's all right," Erin said, "you can tell us both."

"He—he was calling you all kinds of names, and was shakin' me, wantin' to know where you were."

"Are you hurt?" Waite asked.

"No, no, but he scared ten years off my life, he did. And when I couldn't tell him where you'd gone, he went crazy. Throwin' and breakin' things. He tore it up, Missus.''

"What, Annie? What did he tear up?''

"Your beautiful portrait, missus. The one in the ballroom.'' Annie stepped sideways and pointed to the bed. "He told me to bring it here. And all these other possessions of yours. And he wants this room locked up forever. He left the mansion. I'm wonderin' if you shouldn't do the same, missus. I wouldn't want to think of what he might do, were he to see you again.''

"Oh, God. No!'' Erin cried, stumbling toward the bed. Her heart hammering in her chest, she touched the ruined canvas. Surrounding it on the bed were other pictures of her, jewelry, even a small sculpture of one of Della's beloved Thoroughbreds. "Oh, Waite,'' she said, looking at him over her shoulder. "What am I going to do?''

He dismissed Annie, then hurried to Erin's side. The portrait had been viciously slashed with a knife, just as the maid had said.

"You can't even see the locket. It's as if it wasn't painted into the portrait at all. Oh, God, what am I going to do?''

"I'm so sorry, Erin.'' But was he really? This meant she couldn't leave, didn't it? It meant she would have to stay here—with him. One look at her devastated expression filled him with guilt. There had to be some way, he thought, to get her back to her time. He couldn't keep her here, no matter how much he wanted it. He picked up the other pictures of Della that lay nearby.

"Maybe she's wearing the locket in one of these," he said, but quickly discovered that wasn't the case. He shook his head. "That might not work, anyway. Maybe the magic, or whatever it is, is in this portrait alone. And now that Della is...gone, the portrait can't even be copied."

Erin's eyes widened. She grasped his arm. "But I'm here, Waite...and I look just like her," she said, excitement slipping into her voice. "It's a long shot, but it's the only one I've got. The man who painted this portrait, does he live in Munro?"

"No. But he's still here," Waite said. "He's in the artist's studio. J.B.'s paying the man to paint landscapes for me."

Erin raced to the closet, flinging it open and searching through the dresses that hung there. "It's here!" she shouted. "The dress she wore to sit for the portrait. Thank God," she exclaimed, rushing back to his side. "This could work, Waite. It just might work!"

CHAPTER SIXTEEN

WAITE HAD ONLY BEEN GONE fifteen minutes when Erin heard the bedroom door open. She came out of the bathroom, tucking her denim shirt into the waistband of her jeans, and saw J.B. standing in the middle of the room.

When he spotted her, his skin went parchment pale, his jaw slackened and he shook his head.

"J.B.!" He looked as if he was on the verge of a stroke. "Are you all right?"

He backed away from her. "You...you're dead...." He blinked red-rimmed eyes, then rubbed at them with the heel of one hand, still edging backward. "You were dead...in the cave...."

Oh, God. He'd found Della's body. "J.B., listen to me. I...I'm not her. I tried to tell you that the night I came out of the tunnels." She moved toward him.

His back hit the wall, and his eyes were wide, dazed. He shook his head again. "Not...her? But you... If you're not her, who—?"

As angry as Erin had been with him over his mistreatment of Della, she felt sympathy for him now. It was obvious from his red, swollen eyes that he'd grieved for his wife. And now it seemed he thought he was seeing her ghost. She took slow steps to his side. When she placed a hand on his arm, he flinched, then stared down at it as though wondering if it was real flesh and blood.

"Come on, J.B., let's get you over to this chair," she said. "Having a stroke at forty-something isn't your destiny. Trust me on this."

She got him seated, then knelt in front of him and took a deep breath. "You're not seeing Della's ghost. My name is Erin Sawyer. And you're going to find this impossible to believe, but..."

FRANKLIN HAD WATCHED Della's companion leave by the front door, then waited another forty-five minutes until he was sure the man wouldn't be waltzing back in. His palms had begun to sweat as he stood in the shadows, and his nerve had nearly deserted him. But he forced himself to think about Henry, to remember the obscene image of his sweet, sensitive brother lying in the coffin. It was all the incentive he needed to move out of the shadows and up to the mansion.

Stealing inside, he made a quick survey of the empty foyer, then strode toward the first parlor. He froze when he heard Della's voice, then a man answering her, and ducked inside the room until he saw them go past. Peering out at them, he watched as they walked toward the ballroom.

"It's simply too hard to believe," he heard the man say.

"But it's true, J.B. You saw the money, the driver's license. And you saw *her*. When Waite returns, he'll back me up on what happened in Missouri. He read the name on those papers, too." There was a pause, then, "You owe it to her to read the diary. You'll understand why she..."

Her voice faded as they rounded a corner. Franklin crept after them, keeping a careful eye out for servants. His luck held the entire way into the ballroom. Hiding behind a massive chair, he watched as the pair bent down, then entered the fireplace. Keys were rattled, then a door scraped open. It closed behind them.

Franklin glanced around the enormous ballroom one more time before heading toward the door in the fireplace. If his hunch was right, J.B. and Della Munro had just entered the tunnels through an entrance other than the one he knew about...the one Della had taken him through when she'd been so anxious to hear news of Henry, whom she had thought was still alive.

Della and J. B. Munro had killed him. Both of them. And Franklin no longer cared if there was one body or two left behind in the tunnels. J. B. Munro, he decided, was just as guilty as his wife. He took the gun out of his pocket and quietly opened the door.

IT WAS THERE AT THE bottom of the concrete steps, as Erin had known it would be. She leaned down and picked it up, showing it to J.B., who hovered at her shoulder. "See? Just as I told you. The chain broke when I fell and hit my head."

"I remember this locket now. Waite gave it to her." He frowned. "How could a piece of jewelry and a portrait..."

"I don't know," she whispered, and wondered why she felt no joy at finding the locket. Here it was, finally, in her hands. Her ticket home. Or at least, half of the ticket. The portrait would have to be duplicated, and even then, she couldn't be sure it would work.

But if it did, she would step back into her time, back to her family, her job—her reality. Three days ago, she would have done handstands over finding this small bit of gold. Now she'd almost trade it for a birth certificate with an earlier date on it—one that matched Waite MacKinnon's.

She felt guilty at the thought. When had her pop's health ceased to become the most important thing to her?

"You said you saw what he looked like," J.B. said, interrupting her thoughts. "I'll need a description for the police before you go."

"Yes, of course. I hadn't thought—"

"There'll be no describing," a curt voice declared from the top of the stairs.

Erin gave a startled shriek. She bumped shoulders with J.B. when they spun around.

"Who are you?" J.B. demanded.

"Ask your wife." He pointed the deadly little gun in his hand at Erin. "She and I met just days ago. A very memorable meeting."

J.B.'s gaze flicked to hers. "You know him?"

"I'm not her, remember?" Erin whispered. She squinted up at the man, not able to make out his features because of the glare cast by the naked bulb beside him. The gun in his hands gave her a good indication of who the man was, if not his name, and she shivered.

"Is it him?" J.B. murmured.

"I expect so. But he had a beard—it was the only thing I could make out clearly that night."

He stepped in front of the light, and Erin's gasp echoed off the tunnel walls. Her father's features. Only hard . . . angry.

"Let's move away from this door," he ordered, waving the gun as he came down the steps toward them.

Erin didn't budge. "Who are you?" she asked, though she had an inkling, now that she'd seen the striking resemblance. But if she was going to die, and it appeared that she was, she at least wanted to know the man's name and why he had killed her grandmother. She'd been through too much to have the last piece of the puzzle withheld from her now.

"Very funny. You heard me, Della, move!"

"No. Not until I know." She was shaking, frightened of the gun and the man who wielded it, but he was going to tell her, damn it. "You'll have to shoot me here. And you don't want to do that so close to the door, where someone in the house might hear. You tell me, and I'll move."

"You look familiar," J.B. put in, placing a protective hand on Erin's arm. The man was only three feet from them now. "Who—"

He swung the gun on J.B. "I ought to look familiar to you, you bastard, since my brother and I could be twins. But then, you destroy so many lives, it's hard to remember one victim from the next, I suppose. Start walking."

"Your brother?" Erin prompted, stalling, refusing to move when J.B. tugged at her arm. She knew who his brother was now, of course. If he looked so much like the man with the gun, then he could be no one other than the father of Della's child...her own grandfather. And this man was her father's uncle. She'd been a bit slow on the uptake, but forgave herself under the circumstances. "What's happened to Henry? Why do you want to kill us because of him?" she asked, again stalling for time.

"Don't you dare speak his name," the man ground out, his face mottled, his mouth twisted. "You killed him, and I won't let you speak his name again...or see his child ever again."

"Henry," J.B. breathed, obviously clued in by the man's last statement. "He's dead?"

"By your hands just as surely as his own."

"Oh, God, no..." Erin closed her eyes, remembering Della's description of the man from her diary. He'd been kind and courageous, honorable and deeply religious. He'd loved Della, no matter what, and he'd been the only one to ever tell her she was beautiful. "He...committed suicide."

"And over you!" the man spat out. "He took his life because he couldn't live another day without a whore like you!"

Erin's rage was an instantaneous fire in her blood. No! Della wasn't a whore! Erin knew what living in Della's skin felt like now, and whether it was that empathy or a protective familial instinct, she couldn't stand to hear the woman maligned so viciously. Henry, her love, wouldn't stand for it, either. Her anger didn't allow room for common sense.

"Don't call her that! She loved him. And your brother loved her."

His hand shot out and delivered a brutal slap to her face. Her back was slammed against the hard tunnel wall, and she heard the clatter of the gun as he threw it to the floor. In the next moment, his hands were around her throat, and his eyes gleamed with murderous intent.

She could hear J.B.'s shouts echoing off the walls, even glimpsed him out of the corner of her eye, struggling to pull the man off her. But he was no match for Thomas's unholy wrath. Erin struggled for breath, pushed and slapped at the man's arms, but felt herself weakening. Her vision filled with dancing spots of color, and she knew she was about to lose consciousness . . . knew that she was going to die as Della had died.

Then suddenly his hands fell away from her throat, and the crushing weight of his body was lifted off her. She slid to the floor, coughing and gasping for air. Tears streamed from her eyes, and when she looked up, she expected to see J.B. But it was Waite who stood there, the gun in his hand, its butt facing outward. He'd obviously knocked Thomas senseless with it.

He shoved the gun into J.B.'s hand and was kneeling beside her in the space of a heartbeat. "Erin," he murmured, his voice hoarse. "God, Erin." Then he clutched her to his chest, running his hands over her back, her arms, tangling them in her hair as he rocked her back and forth.

"You weren't there when I came back. I looked all through the mansion...every room. Then I saw the padlock on the floor and thought you'd come down here alone. God, do you know what it did to me, seeing his hands on you? I thought I'd lost you.... I couldn't bear that."

Her throat was raw and her head ached. As she clung to him, she wept harsh, bitter tears for all the heartbreak, all the sorrow that had been suffered by Della and Henry, even for Henry's brother's pain and J.B.'s loss. And she cried for Waite and herself. They were connected to all the others in this bizarre and tragic soap opera, yet they were separate, as well. It seemed as if their relationship would mirror Henry and Della's—two people who loved each other, but weren't allowed to be together.

Erin saw the oval locket on the floor next to her where it must have dropped during the struggle, and with trembling fingers and a shattered heart, she reached to pick it up. She closed her eyes then,

pressing her face against his shirt and grasping
fistfuls of the fabric in her hands.

"I found it, Waite," she said, and began to sob
again. "I found the damned locket."

"HOW AM I EXPECTED to duplicate the portrait
when she constantly fidgets, Mr. Munro?" The
artist glared at Erin. She rolled her eyes, eliciting a
grin from J.B. "Your wife, she could sit still. Why
can't the sister?"

"Falvo," he said, gazing at the portrait over the
artist's shoulder, "You of all people should know
a thing or two about temperament. They might
look uncannily similar but Erin here is nothing like
her . . . sister."

"It's true," Erin said, protective feelings for
Della surfacing at J.B.'s remark. "I fidget, she
didn't. I can't sit a horse, she was an expert rider.
She had a wonderful sense of style and fashion, I
can't tell a Chanel from a Lanvin. She was free-
spirited—"

"You've made your point," J.B. said with a
grudging smile, then came from behind the artist
around to Erin's side.

Falvo groaned and threw his hands in the air.
"The light, Mr. Munro, you're blocking my light!
You give me instructions. 'It must be exactly like
the first portrait, Falvo. The tone, the mood, the

light, Falvo. Falvo, duplicate, duplicate, duplicate! And by the way, Falvo, we need it within the week.' I ask you, is my job not difficult enough without someone always fidgeting or moving into my light?"

"All right, Falvo." J.B. moved to Erin's other side. "He needs a Valium," he whispered, borrowing the phrase Erin had used on him just yesterday as he'd paced back and forth behind the artist.

"Stop that. You'll make me laugh."

"You *have* made your point, you know," he said, his tone serious now. "You and Waite...the diary. I have much to answer for."

"Yes, J.B., you do."

"I look around me, see all these *things* I thought were so important and I feel small, ashamed. It was family I should have cherished, people who should have come first. Della especially. God, how she must have hated me."

"I'm sure she did at times. *I* did after reading what she wrote. But, J.B., if I didn't think there was hope for you, I wouldn't have shown you the diary. I wouldn't have thought it would make a difference."

She risked Falvo's temper and turned to J.B. with a soft smile. "You do know how to be generous. I saw a glimpse of it the night that woman crashed the dinner party and you told me she and her children would be taken care of, no matter what, and in—"

Falvo broke in with another of his groans.

"Oh, take a pill, Falvo. I'll turn around in a minute!"

J.B. chuckled.

"I've seen it," she continued, "in your relationship with Waite and in your efforts to make this town's economy thrive. J.B., it's not just your empire that concerns you, you can't convince me of that. You care about the people of this town."

"But where was that concern when it came to Della? I treated her— God, I never realized what my actions were doing to her. I thought good old-fashioned discipline was the way to raise a child. My father was a stern man, and I turned out all right."

"Did you, J.B.?"

He lowered his eyes. "I thought so, but now . . ."

"J.B., look at me." She waited until his troubled eyes met hers. "The biggest mistake you could make now is to come away from all this not having learned anything. You were wrong to treat Della as you did—your priorities were sadly misplaced. But at least you realize it now, and feel remorseful. But now you have to go on, stop wallowing in guilt and get on with your life."

"And what will that life be like now?" he asked. "I've lost everyone, Erin. Della ... Waite ... even you will leave tomorrow."

The mention of Waite's name and her pending departure tore at her heart. She hadn't seen him for two days—not since he'd come to tell her goodbye. Unlike J.B., he hadn't been intimidated into moving from her side by the temperamental artist's ravings. He had stood his ground, not caring who heard what he'd had to say to her.

"I love you, Erin Sawyer," he'd said. "And I wanted to tell you that for years to come." He'd glanced away for a moment, his strong throat working, then had looked back with dark, anguished eyes. "What I'd give to be able to go with you... But I can't. I thought seeing you again would hurt too much, but I knew I had to come— to say the words again—for all the times I won't be able to tell you...."

"I'm sorry," J.B. said, and his tone was sincere. He brushed away a tear from the corner of Erin's eye. "I'm not the only one who'll be alone, am I?"

"No, you aren't." She blinked back more tears. "But, J.B., you have a lot of years ahead of you. That much I know. You can either bemoan your fate and become a miserable old man, or you can take what you've learned and change your ways."

She grinned up at him. "Somehow, I just don't see you as a bemoaning-his-fate kind of guy."

"Thank you," he murmured. "For everything."

"You'll do okay," she assured him, then rose from the chair she'd been sitting in for too many hours. "Falvo," she said, rotating her head in circles to relax as she came around to where he stood behind the portrait. "That's all I can take for now. I'm— Oh!"

"Oh! That's all you have to say is, 'Oh!' " he exclaimed, glaring at her over his shoulder.

"It's...amazing. Exactly like the other one, isn't it?"

She reached to touch it, and Falvo batted at her hand. "Uh-uh-uh! You want to smudge it?"

She jerked her hand back, but not because the artist had taken her to task. The humming sound. She'd heard it again just now as her fingers had neared the canvas. It was going to work, she thought miserably. It was really going to work.

"Are you ill, Erin?" J.B. asked.

She glanced up at him, saw his concern. "No...I...I'll be fine."

She strode out of the room, wondering if she really would be fine. Could she find the strength of will to follow the advice she had given J.B. and just get on with her life?

"ALL FINISHED THEN, Falvo?" J.B. asked, strolling over to take another look.

"Yes, she's finished. Again."

"Well, it's remarkable. Just like the first one. You're a genius, as I've said before."

"Yes. So you have. And so I am." He gazed at his work for a quiet moment, then sighed. "I didn't thank you for requesting the piece be replaced. It is an honor to know one's work is held in such high esteem. Though I suspect your lovely wife's memory also motivated the request."

"Yes, I wanted it for that reason, too." For Erin's trip back, but also in Della's memory.

J.B. cocked his head. "Falvo...this shadow," he murmured, pointing to the grayish area that struck Erin's shoulder.

"Yes?"

J.B. shook his head. "Never mind. I'm sure it was there in the first one, as well."

"Of course," Falvo stated firmly. Then he turned back to putting his materials away.

"Good. Thank you again."

Falvo watched the tycoon leave the room, then rolled his eyes. *Falvo, it must be exact, Falvo, the same lighting!* He was an artist, not a machine. How could the words that had come from Waite MacKinnon's heart not be included some way in the portrait? If only in the shadow he had cast.

ERIN GAZED UP AT the mural one last time. She would see it again, of course, and in its finished form. Still, she'd had to have one last look at it now—in the twenties. She had spent the entire morning taking last looks. The parlors, the kitchens, the gardens. She had even trekked out to look at the Packard one last time.

"I see you're dressed for travel."

Erin's gaze flew to J.B., who stood in the doorway of the ballroom. "Yes. I'm going back now."

"He's leaving today, too."

She had accepted her loss. There were no tears left. "You've talked to him," she said, oddly calm.

"I have. He wants to travel but doesn't know where. Sounds more like aimless wandering to me." He sighed. "But he concedes that his travels might lead him back here one day. He might come home to play the gentleman rancher, of all things."

"That wouldn't be so bad, would it?" she asked, as he came toward her. "Remember what you've learned. Your business relationship isn't as important as your personal ties. He's your friend first, J.B. And at least you'd have him close by."

He smiled, and took her hand. "I'll miss you, Erin. But you say I'll see you again?"

"Yes. You'll see me again." The humming noise sounded, and Erin frowned, looking back over her shoulder at the portrait. "Do you hear that, J.B.?"

"Hear what, dear?"

"That noise, the humming... It's what I heard just before I blacked out in the tunnel."

"No, I don't hear anything."

"Well, I suppose my ride's here."

She looked up at him again. One last time, she thought, just one last time. She reached up with her fingertips and gently touched the faint silver scar. "I recognized you when I first got here by this scar, you know."

J.B. lifted his fingers to the scar, a smile curving his lips. "Della did that. She threw a plate at me when I canceled her trip to Europe."

Erin grinned, then grew solemn. "Be happy, J.B. And tell Waite... tell him I—"

"Erin!"

Her words froze in her throat and she looked toward the doorway where he stood. He was dressed in the pants and wool shirt he'd worn the day of their first kiss, his face ruddy, his hair windblown. Her pulse began to race in time with the sound of the humming in her ears.

"I'll leave you now, Erin." She could barely hear J.B. over the noise that was growing louder by the moment. "Goodbye, dear. I'm most grateful." Then he kissed her cheek and was gone.

Waite strode forward, a desperate light shining in the black depths of his eyes. "Not yet," she thought she heard him say. "Don't go yet."

When he stood before her, the scent of leather and horse and the outdoors enveloped her, and memories came flooding back. That first day, the 101 Ranch, the sight of him at the dinner party, so devastatingly handsome in evening clothes. *How can I leave you?* she thought mournfully, but knew the choice was not hers to make.

"I have to go now, Waite." She raised her voice to be heard. "You know that."

"I know," he said loudly. "But I had to see you one last time. I rode Cherokee this morning and thought about ways I could make this not happen. I thought of carrying you away from here, taking you with me . . . somewhere . . . anywhere."

She squeezed her eyes shut, the humming almost unbearable, her grief just as strong. "But you can't. I . . . love you," she said. "I'll always—"

"What?"

She opened her eyes, looked up at him with a frown.

"I can't hear you, Erin. Say it louder."

"Waite! Oh, God! You can hear it?" She grabbed his forearms. "J.B. couldn't hear it. But you can. . . ."

He frowned. "What is it? It's as loud as a damned train."

It was. And he could hear it! Joy rocketed through her at the possibility. She threw her arms around his neck and kissed him. "I think it means you get to come with me!" she shouted. "Remember, history has it that you were never heard from again. Maybe it's possible. I can't stay, but maybe you can—"

He gaped at her, then at the portrait.

"Unless... Waite, is it what you want? You'd be leaving everything you've ever known, every-one—"

He shook his head, still stunned, but smiling. "I want to be where you are." And he didn't have to shout it for Erin to hear every word.

Her heart pumping wildly, she grabbed his hand and they walked toward the portrait. When they stood inches away, she glanced heavenward, sending up a prayer. *Please. Please, let it work.* She locked gazes with him. "Touch my locket, and the one on the canvas, Waite. At the same time." She swallowed. "If it doesn't work... If you stay behind... I lo—"

He cut off her words with a blistering kiss, rife with promises of a love strong enough to survive the decades. "It will work," he said against her mouth. And she believed him.

She looked back at the ballroom again. For the last time. Imagining it as it had been that first night, she heard the bright jazz music, saw the people mingling and laughing, dancing beneath the Waterford crystal chandelier. She shook her head in wonder. A place out of time, out of history books and museums—J.B. and Della's world—and she had been allowed to experience it, to live it, if only for a little while.

She turned to Waite, ready now. Lifting his hand to her locket, she placed her own fingertips there, as well, then felt the compulsion to touch the canvas. Waite felt it, too, she could tell. Just before darkness took her, she thought she heard the faint voice of J.B. Saying goodbye.

EPILOGUE

IF THERE WAS A SIGHT more breathtaking than Waite MacKinnon in jeans and a chest-hugging Western shirt as he rode a stallion that loved racing over the Oklahoma prairie as much as his rider, Erin had never seen it. She loved watching her new husband take the horse through its paces, loved the gift of time they'd been given. It was a gift she gave thanks for every day of her life.

Waite needed the outlet his morning rides gave him. Though he never complained, the strain of adjusting to this strange new world was beginning to get to him. He was doing well in the business courses he'd enrolled in at the community college, but only Erin and the few members of her family who knew Waite's true birthdate understood what a struggle it was for him. He labored long and hard over the books, grappling with assignments made more difficult because his knowledge of business was from another era. He spent hours at the library, soaking up history, technology and science—all the advances and events that had come after the 1920s.

He claimed it was fascinating, and Erin knew he was being honest for the most part. But she also realized he wasn't doing it for himself. He was intent upon making a good living for them, and he'd learned quickly that in 1994, farming or ranching would require a huge amount of capital for start-up. And his chances of becoming a success, or even making a decent living for her and the family he so desperately wanted were tenuous at best. So he'd decided his future would be in business. Never mind that it wasn't what he loved doing, he'd insisted; it was what he was good at.

Stubborn, stubborn man, she thought, smiling as she watched him head the stallion back to the corral for the hundredth try at teaching the horse various tricks she'd seen at the Wild West show. Cherokee, The Sequel, as she had dubbed his stallion, was having none of it, but Waite wouldn't give up. Waite MacKinnon, she had learned, gave the word *stubborn* a whole new meaning. He spotted Erin standing near the railing of the corral and his lips split in a roguish smile. He trotted Cherokee over and did a fancy trick-rider dismount, then bowed with a flourish. "Bow," he muttered out of the side of his mouth to Cherokee. "Come on, bow!"

Erin laughed. Waite dropped the reins and sauntered over to her. He pulled her up on tiptoe, and she ran her fingers through his sweat-damp hair, pulling his head down for a deep, lusty kiss. "You are such a show-off," she murmured against his lips, then dropped her hands to the first mother-of-pearl snap on his shirt. "And too sexy for this shirt."

He chuckled, and tipped her chin for another morning kiss. "Do you plan to undress me in public, woman? In *my* day, flappers and bathtub gin were shocking. Dresses above the knee and rolled-down stockings, petting parties at college. But I'm telling you, the world's gone to hell in a handbasket. I like rock and roll, but why they have to sing it in their underclothes, and dance around imitating—well, you know—I'll never understand. And stop laughing. It would be a culture shock to anyone who—"

"Came from my day," Erin finished for him, a mischievous twinkle in her eyes. "Do you know how funny it is to hear my father's words coming out of your mouth?"

"I live to amuse," he said dryly, trying out a smart-aleck comment she'd taught him just that week. "How was that?"

"Very good," she praised. "I'll have you caught up to the nineties by the end of the decade, I think."

"Straight up?"

She giggled and gave him a thumbs-up sign, then melted when he dragged her into his embrace and lowered his mouth to hers. Rock and roll and modern lingo was forgotten, Cherokee was ignored, the rest of world faded as the kiss quickly changed from teasing to sensual. Erin was unsnapping more mother-of-pearl snaps, when the sound of a car engine interrupted.

Waite broke the kiss, frowning curiously at the expensive car as it bounced and jutted along the dirt road that led to the small farmhouse and acreage outside Munro that Aunt Shirley had given them as a wedding present. The man who climbed out of the sedan was dressed in a suit and balanced a huge arrangement of flowers and a briefcase in his hands.

"Are you Erin MacKinnon?" he called out as he walked toward them. Erin eyed the flowers in puzzlement, then turned to Waite with a smile. "You sweetie, you. What's the occasion?"

Waite shrugged. "Not from me," he replied, his forehead creasing. "Maybe they're from your mom and pop. Strange, though. He doesn't look like a deliveryman. He looks more like one of those Yuppie businessmen you're always warning me I'd better not turn into."

Erin nodded. "He does, doesn't he?" she whispered. "And Pop wouldn't send flowers, he'd bring some out of his own garden." Her pop was in the best of health these days, having recovered from the last attack quite well while Erin had been "gone." He'd become an avid gardener since recuperating, as well as a genealogy hound. Erin and Waite's story had been difficult to believe at first, but once they'd convinced him, he spent all his free time away from the garden researching the family he'd never known he belonged to.

"Yes, I'm Erin," she said finally, and took the bouquet out of the man's hands, poking around for a card.

The stranger chuckled and shook his head. "Oh, you won't find a card in there." He held out his hand and Erin shook it. "My name is Bradford Tompkins. I'm one of the partners in the legal firm of Tompkins, Tompkins, Tompkins and O'Brien." He turned to Waite, shaking his hand, as well. "I'm hoping you're her husband?"

"Yes," Waite answered, his tone uneasy and his gaze narrowed. Aunt Shirley had solved Waite's identity problem, but not through legal channels by any stretch of the imagination. He now had a social security number that allowed him to attend college.

"Good, good." Tompkins opened his briefcase, drawing out a sheaf of papers. On top of it was a sealed envelope bearing Erin's name, printed in bold letters. "I've gotta tell you, I've looked forward to today for some time now. I'm not good with surprises or mysteries. I was always the kid who couldn't resist sneaking a peek at the Christmas presents when my parents weren't home."

"Mysteries?" Erin asked. "What's this all about?"

He smiled. "These flowers are from J. B. Munro."

Her sudden intake of breath matched Waite's stunned expression. "How...I mean..."

The attorney nodded. "I know. He died more than two years ago. My firm represents his estate. We were his legal representatives before his death, too. In fact, he's responsible for my grandfather starting the firm in the first place. Paid for his education, but that's another story.

"Anyway, the estate was settled two years ago except for one matter. This envelope. He instructed that it remain sealed until you married."

"Oh, my God," she murmured, locking gazes with her husband. Her fingers trembled as she took the envelope from the attorney. "From J.B., Waite," she said, barely able to open the envelope. Finally she managed it, pulling out a handsome, yet brittle, sheet of stationery. She grasped Waite's hand and they both read the letter.

Dear Erin and Waite:

I have spent many years with you in my heart and my thoughts. I have wondered how I might help you both and have, I hope, come up with a solution. I instructed my attorneys not to deal with this last portion of my estate until you, Erin, had married. I felt quite certain that would happen fairly soon after you and Waite returned. I want you to set aside your pride and accept this gift. It is my only way to thank you both for the gifts you have given me. Waite, I know you, son. And I have finally come to understand that you weren't happy in the world I brought you into. Take the money and start that ranch, my friend. And Erin... be happy, dear girl. You wished the same for me. And I was. Jonathan Bartholomew Munro, Munro, Oklahoma, 1980.

Erin folded the letter and met Waite's eyes, hers misty with tears and his moist, as well. He glanced over at the attorney.

Tompkins handed Erin a check, then grinned when her eyes widened at the amount. More than enough, she thought, to start five ranches.

"I was curious to meet you, Mrs. MacKinnon. I knew most of Mr. Munro's friends and acquaintances, but hadn't known about you. I was especially interested because of the amount of that check."

"Her... grandmother," Waite said, "was someone very important to J.B."

"Ah." The attorney nodded. "He was quite a generous man. As I said, my grandfather didn't know him well, yet Mr. Munro paid for his education. Well... congratulations on your marriage." He shook their hands again. "It's off to a good start, eh?"

When Tompkins left, Waite enfolded Erin in his arms.

"He was happy," Erin said, and held her husband closer. "I was worried about that, you know."

"Me too. Me too."

Erin glanced up at him. "Tompkins... Tompkins... That name sounds so familiar."

Waite smiled. "Does it?"

"It does to you, too?"

"Yep. The woman who came the night of the dinner party... remember her?"

"Yes."

"Her husband worked for Munro MacKinnon. Roy Tompkins."

Erin frowned. "But I thought he took a powder... left the family. I can't imagine J.B. sending the jerk to law school."

"He wouldn't have. But you said J.B. assured you he would take care of the woman and her children. I'll bet it was one of her sons he put through college."

"Yes...of course. And you," she said, pointing a finger at Waite's chest. "I know you. You're just like him. The wheels are already turning in that brain of yours. You're trying to figure out who to give this money to, aren't you?"

He grinned. "Some of it. But you know what else I'm thinking?"

She shook her head.

He lifted his face heavenward. "Thank you, J.B. You knew what hell computers would be for me!"

And with that, he handed Erin the check and lifted her in his arms. "Come on," he said, "let me teach you how to ride a horse. You're going to have to learn now."

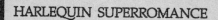

HARLEQUIN SUPERROMANCE

COMING NEXT MONTH

#622 KIM & THE COWBOY • Margot Dalton
Class of '78
Kim Tanaka loves her new studio, but it's too big and expensive.
Enter cowboy Todd McAllister to share the space and the rent.
Todd is different from anyone Kim has ever known—he's large,
loud and lovin'...and eager to share more than the studio with her.
But their respective families have reason to keep the couple apart.
Especially at Christmas....

#623 CATCH A FALLING STAR • Tracy Hughes
Showcase
Laura Rockford, a proverbial poor little rich girl, revels in the
attentions of Zane Berringer, even though the famed country-and-
western singer is bad news when it comes to beautiful young
women. Sly Hancock, Berringer's record producer, knows very
well how his boss operates. He knows it's simply a matter of time
before Laura's heart will be broken. And he plans on sticking
close—very close—to pick up the pieces.

#624 NO CURE FOR LOVE • Tara Taylor Quinn
He's tried for ten years to forget her: Marie Richmond, his
one-time student and protégée. But Pete Mitchell has learned the
hard way that there "ain't no cure for love." Now Marie's devel-
oped an antidote that's being used to blackmail the government.
Lives are at risk—and so is Pete Mitchell's heart.

#625 THE THIRD CHRISTMAS • Margot Early
Family Man
Three years before, there was no Christmas for David Blade and
his young son. That was the year Skye died.... Now it's December
again, and Jean Young becomes part of their lives—and falls in
love with them both, the father and the little boy. She knows her
love can heal them, renew their hope and their happiness.
Especially at Christmas....

HARLEQUIN SUPERROMANCE®

From award-winning author Terri Herrington—
writing for us as **Tracy Hughes**—
comes a special new book.

A Superromance *Showcase* book.

Catch a Falling Star

From Nashville to Nowhere...

Heiress Laura Rockford has made a mess of her life. With the
help of her manipulative mother, her marriage to a washed-up
recording artist disintegrates—and in the blink of an eye she
finds herself divorced, in debt and struggling to make her way
in the country-music business.

And back again!

When Laura hooks up with top recording engineer Sly Hancock,
things begin to change.... For Laura. And for Sly.

Catch a Falling Star is a classic riches-to-rags-to-riches story.
It's intensely emotional, gritty, glamorous—and above all,
romantic. *Catch this star!*

Available in December, wherever
Harlequin books are sold.

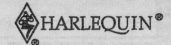

VOWS
Margaret Moore

Legend has it that couples who marry in the Eternity chapel are destined for happiness. Yet the couple who started it all almost never made it to the altar!

It all began in Eternity, Massachusetts, 1855.... Bronwyn Davies started life afresh in America and found refuge with William Powell. But beneath William's respectability was a secret that, once uncovered, could keep Bronwyn bound to him forever.

Don't miss **VOWS,** the exciting prequel to Harlequin's cross-line series, **WEDDINGS, INC.,** available in December from Harlequin Historicals. And look for the next **WEDDINGS, INC.** book, *Bronwyn's Story,* by Marisa Carroll (Harlequin Superromance #635), coming in March 1995.

"HOORAY FOR HOLLYWOOD" SWEEPSTAKES

HERE'S HOW THE SWEEPSTAKES WORKS

OFFICIAL RULES — NO PURCHASE NECESSARY

To enter, complete an Official Entry Form or hand print on a 3" x 5" card the words "HOORAY FOR HOLLYWOOD", your name and address and mail your entry in the pre-addressed envelope (if provided) or to: "Hooray for Hollywood" Sweepstakes, P.O. Box 9076, Buffalo, NY 14269-9076 or "Hooray for Hollywood" Sweepstakes, P.O. Box 637, Fort Erie, Ontario L2A 5X3. Entries must be sent via First Class Mail and be received no later than 12/31/94. No liability is assumed for lost, late or misdirected mail.

Winners will be selected in random drawings to be conducted no later than January 31, 1995 from all eligible entries received.

Grand Prize: A 7-day/6-night trip for 2 to Los Angeles, CA including round trip air transportation from commercial airport nearest winner's residence, accommodations at the Regent Beverly Wilshire Hotel, free rental car, and $1,000 spending money. (Approximate prize value which will vary dependent upon winner's residence: $5,400.00 U.S.); 500 Second Prizes: A pair of "Hollywood Star" sunglasses (prize value: $9.95 U.S. each). Winner selection is under the supervision of D.L. Blair, Inc., an independent judging organization, whose decisions are final. Grand Prize travelers must sign and return a release of liability prior to traveling. Trip must be taken by 2/1/96 and is subject to airline schedules and accommodations availability.

Sweepstakes offer is open to residents of the U.S. (except Puerto Rico) and Canada who are 18 years of age or older, except employees and immediate family members of Harlequin Enterprises, Ltd., its affiliates, subsidiaries, and all agencies, entities or persons connected with the use, marketing or conduct of this sweepstakes. All federal, state, provincial, municipal and local laws apply. Offer void wherever prohibited by law. Taxes and/or duties are the sole responsibility of the winners. Any litigation within the province of Quebec respecting the conduct and awarding of prizes may be submitted to the Regie des loteries et courses du Quebec. All prizes will be awarded; winners will be notified by mail. No substitution of prizes are permitted. Odds of winning are dependent upon the number of eligible entries received.

Potential grand prize winner must sign and return an Affidavit of Eligibility within 30 days of notification. In the event of non-compliance within this time period, prize may be awarded to an alternate winner. Prize notification returned as undeliverable may result in the awarding of prize to an alternate winner. By acceptance of their prize, winners consent to use of their names, photographs, or likenesses for purpose of advertising, trade and promotion on behalf of Harlequin Enterprises, Ltd., without further compensation unless prohibited by law. A Canadian winner must correctly answer an arithmetical skill-testing question in order to be awarded the prize.

For a list of winners (available after 2/28/95), send a separate stamped, self-addressed envelope to: Hooray for Hollywood Sweepstakes 3252 Winners, P.O. Box 4200, Blair, NE 68009.

CBSRLS

OFFICIAL ENTRY COUPON

"Hooray for Hollywood"
SWEEPSTAKES!

Yes, I'd love to win the Grand Prize — a vacation in Hollywood —
or one of 500 pairs of "sunglasses of the stars"! Please enter me
in the sweepstakes!

This entry must be received by December 31, 1994.
Winners will be notified by January 31, 1995.

Name _____

Address _____ Apt. _____

City _____

State/Prov. _____ Zip/Postal Code _____

Daytime phone number _____
(area code)

Account # _____

Return entries with invoice in envelope provided. Each book
in this shipment has two entry coupons — and the more
coupons you enter, the better your chances of winning!

DIRCBS

OFFICIAL ENTRY COUPON

"Hooray for Hollywood"
SWEEPSTAKES!

Yes, I'd love to win the Grand Prize — a vacation in Hollywood —
or one of 500 pairs of "sunglasses of the stars"! Please enter me
in the sweepstakes!

This entry must be received by December 31, 1994.
Winners will be notified by January 31, 1995.

Name _____

Address _____ Apt. _____

City _____

State/Prov. _____ Zip/Postal Code _____

Daytime phone number _____
(area code)

Account # _____

Return entries with invoice in envelope provided. Each book
in this shipment has two entry coupons — and the more
coupons you enter, the better your chances of winning!

DIRCBS